Paul Smith was born and raised in Dublin. He left school when he was eight. His first job was driving a donkey and coal cart; his last regular job was teaching English at Uppsala in Sweden.

In between he took and left a number of jobs in Ireland and abroad. He worked in factories and on boats, was a news-reader in Canada and costume designer at the Abbey and Gate theatres in Dublin.

He has lived in Australia, France, Italy, Canada and the USA. Other books by Paul Smith include *Come Trailing Blood, Stravaganza, The Stubborn Season,* and *The Countrywoman* (also available in Picador). Until 1975, his work was banned in Ireland.

Also by Paul Smith in Picador

The Countrywoman

Paul Smith

ANNIE

PICADOR

published by **Pan Books**

First published in the United States of America 1972 by The Dial Press, New York
This Picador edition published 1987 by Pan Books Ltd,
Cavaye Place, London SW10 9PG
9 8 7 6 5 4 3 2 1
© Paul Smith 1971, 1972
All rights reserved
ISBN 0 330 29755 4

Printed and bound in Great Britain by
Cox & Wyman Ltd, Reading

For
Donald Hutter
and for
Victor Bonham-Carter

annie

1

"I'll stop me dusky dreaming in a minute," Mrs. Murphy said. "In the meantime, where is this I was?"

"Until that tailor's haphazard walked in, stuck fast on the butt'a my pleasure," Mr. Murphy replied. He eyed me sleepy, heaved over on his shoulder, and closed his eyes. "Gifts," he muttered, "shagging well abandoned."

Dragging back her share of the blankets and coats covering the big iron bed, Mrs. Murphy laughed. "Interrupted him, you did," she said, and grinned sly down at the dark head of her husband on the pillow beside her. "He's lepping now because you landed in just as he was about to add another decca to his night-long rosary." Sighing massive, she lay back among the pillows and between her husband and her youngest daughter, edged in against the wall. "Men's blood never seem to cease striving," she said. With effort, she folded her arms across the wild sweep of her chest and impatiently eased her big breasts into a more comfortable position. "This fella's a shagging Trojan," she said, her voice rough, but not with complaint, and in the room's smoky dusk her creamy, thick flesh and black eyes gleamed soft. "A giant," she said. And, content lathering her voice, made gentle the fat, useless hands, easing the covers up over his shoulders and then over her own naked breasts. "Like Annie, sleeps bolliky, he does," she said.

And so did she. Lazily, she stretched down against the dark, muscular body I'd seen when he turned over.

"Built like a stallion, he is," she said. And he was. And she added, "Thanks be to God." And under the canopy of worn blankets, coats, and rags, her legs moved toward his. "Your mother's up," she said, and gestured with her head to the ceiling.

In the rooms overhead, I could hear my mother, filling the kettle from the zinc bucket she kept covered on a tea chest by the window. I heard her weight on the bare, scrubbed floor, and the sound of the blind being taken off the window and the curtains being drawn. But from the room off the one I was standing in, there wasn't a sound.

"I should get up," Mrs. Murphy said, but I knew she wouldn't, for it was a lip service she paid to the day, every day. "It must be late," she mused.

"It's half past five," I said.

"The shagging middle of the night," Mr. Murphy muttered.

"Will I pull the curtains?" I asked.

Mrs. Murphy gazed, puzzled.

"The curtains," I gestured.

"What! An expose this bastion of rags, bones, and bottles before I need to?"

Her eyes, on a streel of sight, took in the stretch of the bed and the humps the twins made at the foot of it. "Them youngfellas should have beds of their own," she said. Her glance, going past them, went to the fire, still black, the hearth littered with ashes, old shoes, bits of socks, scraps of paper, and chewed bones; and then, moseying from that, went to the mantelpiece, to the lamp lowered to a glimmer hanging from a nail in the wall, and finally found its resting place on me.

"It's this lane," she said accusingly. "And this man," she added. "Between the pair of them, I've given up all resistance to decay." She made a half-hearted effort to tidy back the long stream of hair framing her face. "Is that thing going?" she asked, throwing a look to the clock on the mantelpiece.

I shook my head.

"That clock hasn't stirred itself for the past six months," Mr. Murphy said, and turned over onto his side.

"That isn't the only thing that hasn't stirred itself in the past six months," Mrs. Murphy replied. She glanced at me. "Are you early?"

I shook my head again.

"In that case, the Gipsy better get a move on if she's to get the milk done before youse go for the cinders." She cast a quick look down at her husband, but he seemed to be sleeping. "What I need . . . ," she began.

"What you need is right beside you," Mr. Murphy interrupted. "Spread down now, and I'll give yeh another breath a life."

"I thought you were trying to sleep," Mrs. Murphy snapped.

"How the hell can I when I'm here pushing against a weakness no living man should have to strive against?"

Mrs. Murphy shook her head. "Then he blames me for flinging a child at him every nine months. Says it's how the women of Ireland keep their men."

"An isn't it?" Mr. Murphy asked. "How else do youse do it?"

"We use shagging magic, that's how," Mrs. Murphy

said, and I knew the argument, an old one, would be returned to later in the morning. But for the moment she was content to shelve it, for from the little room now, voices tired and sleepy muttered against each other.

"They're awake," she said. "The oil paintings. Paddy Murphy's sleeping beauties."

And then someone screamed. And Mrs. Murphy's roar followed the scream. And in the stunned hush that came, there was a frantic fluttering, a mingling of sounds, and a laugh, an unmistakable laugh, that tore through the sour air of the room and brought a twist of agonized resignation to Mrs. Murphy's face.

"That's her," she cried. "That's the pagan up now, to disturb the maimed and bewildered with the strength of her hooring trottle. I'll strangle that shagging youngwan," she screamed. But she didn't. Instead, she lay back and, sinking further down into the bed, began suddenly to giggle.

"It's your topper," she said, when she could, by way of explanation. "And coat," she added, and under her the whole bed shook.

"What's wrong with them?" I asked.

"Why, nothing," she said. "An now that you mention it, there isn't a brack in the coat, an sure the hat itself gives you inches." Eyeing me over the bedclothes, she made an attempt at seriousness by trying to stiffen the folds of flesh that were her face. "But who in the name a Jasus gave you them?" she asked.

"I told you," I said.

"I know, but it's gone outa me head."

"Ellen Simms," I said, and stared stony.

She sank back. "Well, honest to Christ. But I'd be afraid a them, for who'd know what the fabric of that coat would be hiding?"

"It's clean," I told her, and saw her glance go with slow speculation over my top hat and swallowtail coat.

"I betcha the bastard wore that died on the job," Mr.
Murphy muttered, and then, raising himself up on his elbow,
surveyed me through narrowed eyes. "Went panting to his
grave with hoors in combat. What's the bet? Hundreds and
thousands a hoors. Probably had to be dug outa some big
blond mot. A big, well-stacked blonde. I can just see her,"
he said dreamy, and lay down again. "Why don't you go?"
he said suddenly.

"Because I'm waiting for Annie," I said, and felt my
mouth harden.

"One of these days you'll be left waiting for Annie,"
he said. "One a these days you'll be left like a man on gur
with a murmuring mind. One of these days . . . ," he began,
and broke off. "You *could* wait in the lane," he said.

I *could* and all, but I wasn't going to.

"I wonder if the coat's worth anything?" Mrs. Murphy asked.

I didn't know and I didn't answer. I was thinking
about being left by Annie, thinking about what Mr. Murphy
had said, and suddenly I was filled with a fear that lay like
a stone in the pit of my belly. I heard Mrs. Murphy speak
and saw her stare a question and then heard her say,
"You're not keeping it."

"I am," I told her suddenly.

"And can afford to?" Mrs. Murphy asked.

"It didn't cost me anything," I said, testy, and saw
onto her face the familiar childish wonder creep, that exposed always the slow, laborious mullings of her mind.

"Two—three—maybe even five bob on that coat from
Christy," she said.

And into the calculating mood, the quiet storm that
had been going on in the little room, without either her or
her husband paying any attention to it, she roared sudden.
"Animals!" she shrieked. "Animals!"

The room shuddered, and then a laugh ripped and cut

clean as a knife through the chapel bell ringing out from St. Kevin's. And, from the gray light of the little room, Annie Murphy came, wide-eyed, long-legged, and bolliky.

"I'm up," she said, and her glance swept the room and everything in it.

"You are indeed," Mrs. Murphy said, and let her head back gently. She glared hard. "And I've never yet known you to hansel the day without first ripping the balls out of it."

Annie, on her way to the bed, stopped as if checked. She drew back and, smothering intention, lassoed me with a grin. "It's twinkle-toes," she said quickly. "Thinks I was fecking her sweets."

"And were you?" Mrs. Murphy asked.

"Who, me?" Annie said loud, wanting to be heard in the little room, and, still grinning, held out a fistful of sweets wrapped in different-colored papers. I took some, and so did Mrs. Murphy, and Annie began then to tear through the room for something to wear. She wore as little as possible, and always the worst things she could find. From the line at the fire she took a pair of knickers she had rinsed out the night before, and from under the heads of the twins she pulled a ragged red pinny, and made for the door.

"Not that way!" Mrs. Murphy screamed. "Put something on ya!"

"But there's nobody up," Annie cried.

"And don't touch that," Mrs. Murphy roared as Annie went through the door with a clean white towel that had been set aside for Mr. Murphy and ran out to the lane, to the pipe under which, in the midst of breeze or blast, she washed herself every morning.

"Ah, Jasus, what's the use?" Mrs. Murphy sighed hopelessly. "You can't keep a shagging thing with wan a them." She chewed on her sweets, and in the lane Annie, who was twelve that summer and her third youngest daughter, bellowed a protest at the cold of the water; and then, after a few minutes, the balls of her heels could be heard hitting the cobbles as she came charging back.

"Easy!" Mrs. Murphy shrieked, but Annie had already slammed the door behind her. "You'd waken the shagging dead," Mrs. Murphy complained bitter, but Annie ignored her.

"There's a bit of a rack on the ground at the pipe," she said, and flung the towel back on a chair. "A blue wan," she said, and caught the jacket Mrs. Murphy threw her from the bed.

"Belongs to that craw-thumping Jesus," Mrs. Murphy said, "for I saw him in the lane last night. Musta slept beyant in Quale's hall."

"He didn't," I said. "He slept up on our landing. Me mother gave him a jug of tea."

"An had it to give," Mrs. Murphy murmured begrudging.

"Did you know that bed is touching the floor in the middle?" Annie said.

"It's not the only thing touching the floor in the middle," Mrs. Murphy snapped. "C'm'ere," she said, turning her attention to me. "Isn't it a miracle but Berkley lets Jesus sleep on the landing?"

"He doesn't trouble her," Annie said, standing back to get a better view of the bed.

"That's what I mean. Maybe if he did, oul farthing-cunt would cast a more lenient eye on him turning the landing into a boudoir."

"Why?" Annie asked, and added, "I don't see how that would make any difference."

"You wouldn't," Mrs. Murphy replied. "Cause, for all your street running and road wandering, you and that youngfella there are a bit thick."

"Is that so?" Annie laughed. "Well, you know what they say . . ." She went to the mantelpiece and began rooting through the debris littering it.

"I've never known if youse are childer or the leavings of childer," Mrs. Murphy said, her glance hard and critical as always when it fell on Annie.

"An you've never taken the trouble to find out," Annie spoke back over her shoulder. "He has a floating face," she said suddenly, and whatever it was she had been looking for on the mantelpiece, she hadn't found, for she was now down on her knees going through the press of the dresser.

"Who has?" Mrs. Murphy asked.

"Jesus," Annie replied.

"A white, frightened face," I said, remembering the tramp's stony smile in the dark of the landing the night before, and the rare laugh that had the seed of wild weeping in it.

"Of what?" Annie stared up at me. "Maybe we could find out. Ask around. Miz Robey might know."

"You stay away from Miz Robey," Mrs. Murphy warned, "and from that white-maned oul bastard. Lovely cronies yeh have," she said. "Wan a hoorhouse keeper, and the other a madman." She sighed. "Jasus, but this city is crawling with terrible characters—and they're all friends a yours! You don't know a soul that's respectable, right, or decent."

"What's wrong with them?" Annie asked.

"Not a thing," Mrs. Murphy said, "except that they're all shagging freaks. Look at Ellen Simms, with her pipe and her books and her talk. Now if Ellen Simms isn't a man in skirts, I don't know what is. Nobody can tell me she doesn't stand to piss. An what about oul Robey and her house a hoors?—and Mary Doyle and her mother?—an that poet?—ah the wan with the words, and the fractured hands when it comes to the parting of a penny?—an . . ."

"Don't forget the widder," Annie laughed, and flashed a grin at me.

"Ya mean the wan with the veils?" Mrs. Murphy asked.

Annie nodded, and we both waited.

"Now, *her*," Mrs. Murphy began, "I often wonder about."

"What do you wonder?" Annie took from the press the man's tweed cap she sometimes wore and from which the peak had been ripped.

"Ya mean you don't see anything wrong with *her*?" Mrs. Murphy stared wide-eyed at Annie, who stood with her lips parted over her white teeth that she scrubbed with soot. "No, I don't suppose you do," Mrs. Murphy sighed. "You wouldn't bat an eyelid if every wan in this lane sprouted four legs overnight. You're not ordinary," she said, seeming surprised at the idea, "an oul Robey was right about you. She said in a court of law you'd be useless, for nobody would ever be hanged, drawn, or quartered, cause nobody would ever be accused. She also said there was something in ya that for your own peace of mind you'd be better without."

"What did she mean?" Annie questioned, suspiciously.

"I don't know," Mrs. Murphy replied. "I do, but I can't explain. But she was right." She looked at me and, off on a different track, said, "An what confusion was on Ellen Simms to get *him* up like Rockerfella? Now that's something else I don't understand—unless, of course, she wanted to inflict him with delusions a grandeur he'll never recover from."

"What's wrong with him?" Annie eyed me, then her mother.

"With *him*, nothing," Mrs. Murphy said. "An maybe not even the coat an hat, but . . . ," and she paused to stress: "what about the burden of owning them? That's what he has to worry about. Sure the coat alone could lead him to places where no right person could follow, to say nothing at all about the hat." She paused, and then: "Oh, Ellen Simms was up to some badness there, you mark my words."

"Maybe he should get rid a them," Annie said, and her black moody eyes under the ambush of black lashes were grave and suddenly concerned.

"Without hesitation," Mrs. Murphy said, adding, "an not a minute too soon. In fact," she said, and she smiled, "after, I could chance Christy above in the pawn with them."

Annie laughed and threw her weight against the foot of the bed. "I thought so," she said and, bending over the twins, "I knew it wasn't greedy prayers nibbling your mind, the minute you began. Well, he's not parting with them," she said, and her grin matched her mother's. "So you're going to have to exert yourself, Mollser, and find something else to fling across the counter at Christy." She came away from the bed, back to where I stood, at the table in the middle of the room.

"One thing sure," Mrs. Murphy said viciously, "but when you start to earn your living below in Barker's biscuit factory, I won't have to darken the doors of the pawn *or* trouble Christy." She raised her hand and swiped the hair from her face. "Come September and Barker's will be taking on any amount of little girls," she said lightly, and added, "Alleluia."

"I know one little girl they won't be taking on," Annie said roughly, "for I'm not going into any factory," she continued calmly, "an well you know it."

"When the time comes," Mrs. Murphy replied, "*you* won't be consulted."

From the clash of glances, Mrs. Murphy withdrew hers first. "I don't know what you've got against a good job in a good factory," she said mildly.

"Neither do I," Annie said, "but I'm not going into wan." She stood with her shoulders square.

"So what are you going to do?" Mrs. Murphy asked. "For you don't even know your letters——"

"An whose fault is that?" Annie interrupted, but Mrs. Murphy continued as if she hadn't.

"——an you haven't the delicacy or the looks of your sisters. And you're too shagging unbridled to even talk to a fella, let alone do what Florrie Conners did—so you tell us." Her voice slurred rough: "What the hell will you do?"

"I have a plan," Annie said and, raising her chin, drew in her breath like a singer beginning a song.

"Oh, Jasus, not another," Mrs. Murphy cried.

"This wan happens to be different," Annie said.

"So was the last plan," Mrs. Murphy sneered, "an the plan before that, and the dozen others before them. Them were all the plans and contrivances of a genius. Them were all marvelous plans. Wan a them took that youngfella there into Baggot Street hospital with the spike of a railing up his guts—and your plan to supply the shops of Dublin with fruit and flowers looted out of every garden you came across brought your poor father closer to the gates of Mountjoy than he had ever been."

"They were good plans," Annie said, "and only went wrong because other things happened."

"They did indeed," Mrs. Murphy replied. "An like fate kept happening. Happening at my door. Foul-mouthed police kept happening—an men, women, and children banging on it at all hours of the day and night. They kept happening. So did that mob of tramps you banded together to start a new revolution—and the shopkeepers whose tills you were knocking off because you thought they were wallowing in profits they should never have made—and the owners of the orchards where you and Tucker boxed-the-

fox and, not content with just boxing-the-fox, had to uproot
the trees as well, then plant them along the banks of the
canal. An what about your plan to align yourself with the
band a Good Hopers, because you happened to like the
way they preached and the things they preached about—
you thought if you banged the tambourine hard enough,
you'd make your fortune. But this time I'm having no happening, this time I'm having none of your plans. Come September, you and your plans can unfold themselves between
the four high walls of Barker's biscuit factory."

"They'll never hold her," Mr. Murphy said.

"Then the walls of some jail will," Mrs. Murphy muttered. "Jasus," she sighed, "but when I think of the grown
men, women, and police who've come hammering on that
door over the past few years because of her and her plans,
I wonder I'm alive to tell them."

Annie glanced at her mother. "Are you making a cup
a tea?" she asked.

"I'd love wan." Mrs. Murphy smiled away the scald
of bitter contention the factory was between herself and
Annie. "An a cut a bread smothered with lashings a beef
dripping."

"We have none," Annie said.

"I know," Mrs. Murphy replied, "but that doesn't stop
me wanting it."

"And now you're going to ask me to put a bit of paper
and a few sticks under the kettle," Annie said.

"I know better when you're in wan a your humors,"
Mrs. Murphy laughed. "Tucker will."

"Tucker won't." Annie's look told me to stay exactly
where I was.

"He wouldn't be a minute," Mrs. Murphy coaxed.

"An what about the cinders an the milk?" Annie
glared at her mother. "Can you see your face if I came back
here empty-handed?"

"You never have," Mrs. Murphy admitted easy. "I'll say that for you—yourself and Tucker must be the best cinder-pickers in the business."

"I've had to be," Annie said, and dragged what was left of an old chair bed from the corner of the fireplace and from behind it took up a sack. "We should have a box for these," she said, dumping the cinders still in it onto the floor.

"Tell your father," Mrs. Murphy replied coldly.

"I have," Annie said, "and a lot of good it's done."

Mrs. Murphy sagged. "Beyond the regions of this bed, all Paddy Murphy's interests cease." She looked at me. "It isn't, mind, that he won't do something. It's just he's afraid, God help him, of going through life with a bent back."

"He should get a job," Annie said.

"What? An part company with his senses?" Mrs. Murphy shouted, before her eyes snapped fury down at the twins. "Ah, for Christ's sake," she roared, "keep them shagging trotters to yourselves." She gazed at Annie. "Why, it must be all of ten years since your father turned his hand at the manipulation of a shilling, honest or otherwise. And as for your brothers and sisters . . ." She paused. "Well, only a fool would think of calling Alice or Henny robust; an as for Ackle and Con—it's not their fault they can't knock out a living."

"Sure, I know," Annie said. "But what would they do if they didn't have me to knock it out of them . . . ? An what would he do?" she asked, gesturing to her father in the bed.

"Offer me loneliness up," Mr. Murphy shouted. "Shagging kids," he muttered. "Jasus, but that's a terrible troublesome youngwan," he said in peevish complaint; and beside him, Mrs. Murphy nodded her agreement.

"No wonder I don't know me letters," Annie said suddenly. "I should've gone to school."

"There wasn't time," Mrs. Murphy snapped. "How

could I have managed with you shut up in some school all day?"

"How do other people manage?" Annie asked, and, like a gull astray in the lane, began to scavenge the table for something to eat from the littered remains of last night's meal.

"Oh, now there I leave you!" Mrs. Murphy laughed. "But, as for schooling, sure you an Rockerfella there are getting the best a schooling—youse are meeting people, all day, every day, all classes, creeds, and colors. Youse, whether youse know it or not, are on talking terms with the mighty."

"This table's filthy," Annie said.

"An you know who's to blame for that," Mrs. Murphy cried. "Between your brothers and two delicate sisters, I'm nicely hoped up. Honest to Jasus," she said on a sigh, "but be the time you take your departure in the mornings, I don't know whether I'm plum or currant."

"That's because of the mighty effort you put into it," Annie said, but not loud enough for her mother to hear. She bit into the crust in her hand. "What would you say if I quit the milk round?" she asked suddenly.

"Not a thing," Mrs. Murphy replied quietly and, in the bed beside her, Mr. Murphy's eyes climbed over the bedclothes. "Except that you'll do so over my emancipated body," Mrs. Murphy said. "You'll give up the milk round the day you walk into Barker's biscuit factory," she said, "an not a day sooner." And then, into the mute appeal in Annie's eyes, she suddenly blazed. "It's time you grew up," she roared. "You're like a shagging Gipsy with your wandering. Well, it's time at twelve years of age you began to set your mind in line with your spine, and began to behave like every other little girl round the place."

"You're always telling me I'm not like every other little girl round the place," Annie said.

"And you're not," Mrs. Murphy cried. "And you never have been. You don't even look like them."

"How do I look?" Annie asked, and she was suddenly very still, and very quiet.

"Unnatural," Mrs. Murphy said. And then, on a wild burst of anger: "You're like some shagging, savage throwback! I don't know in the name of Jasus where you came from, or what crime it was I committed to be saddled with you, or where it is your wandering's going to land you, for you're at ease with yourself only on the streets."

"That's true," Annie said, while her mother nodded briskly her own satisfaction.

"Well, it's a pity you won't end up on them," Mrs. Murphy said, "but you won't, for if they ever hanged you for being a beauty, you'd die innocent."

I looked at Annie. She stood bony and lanky in her red pinny, and her face, that every summer grew darker than her hair, was white.

"Miz Robey says Annie's not exactly plain, either!" I said. "An the Poet—he says she's a beauty, a jewel on the dowdy streets."

Mrs. Murphy glared at me. "So now you're throwing in your tuppence worth." She paused, and her sudden laugh hacked. "Well, the Poet and the hoorhouse keeper should know," she said.

"Maybe her figure's nothing to write home about," I began, remembering what Miz Robey had said about Annie, "but . . ."

"An neither are her diddies," Mrs. Murphy roared her interruption—and now she was a woman in spite, gregging a fight. "She's about as chicken-chested as you are," she said, and, easing her head back, she narrowed her eyes as if to get me and Annie and the room in focus. "Why, when I was her age, I had hips that could rock canal boats, and breasts a ton weight."

"And still have, thanks be to God," Mr. Murphy said, but she had gone beyond the stage where she could be coaxed out of one mood into another.

"An just look at your sisters," she added, and gestured with her eyes toward the little room.

"Her legs are better than theirs," I said. And so were her shoulders, I thought.

"How the hell would you know?" Mrs. Murphy cried, her glance glazed, her vexation at my interference showing in the rearing of her face up into the gloom hovering over her, and the unframed picture of the sacred heart nailed to the wall.

"Because the chiselers nowadays are getting round to it long before we did," Mr. Murphy said.

"Ah, you were born with a standing prick," Mrs. Murphy shouted. "An that's why sex, and anything to do with sex, is the first thing that crosses your dirty, lecherous oul mind."

"Maybe I'll grow better," Annie said suddenly.

"Maybe," Mrs. Murphy replied, but you could see she had her doubts. "Good legs . . . ," she mused. "Faith, and good legs won't be enough to get you a husband."

"A husband and the factory," Annie said. "That's all I ever hear in this house. Well, I'm not going into any factory and I don't want a husband."

"*Now*, no," Mrs. Murphy said, "but later on you'll want a husband, and unless you intend to end up like Ellen Simms or wan a them other crazy oul bitches you mitch your days away with, you'll start thinking right now. Fix your hair, to begin with, and let it grow as nature intended it to grow. Stop roughing about. Walk, instead a running, that way you'll give your body a chance to fill out an soften up. Quit whistling and sparring up to every youngfella you come across. Speak soft and sweet and give over running from here to the pump every morning bollick naked. An for Christ's sake put shoes on your feet."

"Shoes?" I looked at Annie, who couldn't be bet, bribed, or bullied into wearing shoes, and went barefoot in all weathers.

"An in the mornings, after you've delivered the milk and gathered the cinders," Mrs. Murphy was saying, ". . . come back here!"

"An do what?" Annie asked.

"What every other little girl does," Mrs. Murphy replied, and Annie, who had never been known in her life to do what other girls did, said,

"I'll think about it."

She nudged me to alertness.

"One thing, though," she said, and now her gaze was level with her mother's. "I'm not going into Barker's."

"You," Mrs. Murphy said as we went out the door, "won't have any say in the matter."

2

"That's what she thinks."

In the lane, Annie aimed what was left of the crust in her hand through Nan Oxer's open window. We stood, hoping for repercussions, but there were none.

"Mollser doesn't know it yet," Annie said, "but I'm quitting Nolan's right now and from this morning on I'm doing no more milk rounds." She spoke into the hour, striking from the clock on the steeple of the Town Hall in Rathmine's—and then, as if released from some affliction, jumped and made a swipe at a low-flying gull, and missed. "It was a lousy job," she said, swinging her empty sack across her shoulders, while her eyes, bravely challenging, followed the lurching flight of the gull.

We stood still in the middle of the lane, surrounded by houses parched for whitewash, pockmarked by windows blinded by lace rags and brown paper, and then she ran, and was in the street when I caught up with her, pushing on the doors of the hucksters, in case one of them had been left unlocked. But none of them had. She tried the door of Doyle's, but that didn't budge, either. And then she moved from the door to the window, and stared hard at her reflection in the glass.

"That's funny," she said, but she didn't move.

"What is?" I asked, and from a room in the street came the sound of crying, and it was a grieving baby cry.

"What me Ma said," Annie replied. "About me being ugly."

"It's not the first time," I said.

"I know, and before I've never given much mind to what she had to say about anything, but just lately it's sticking." She backed from the glass. "I feel sick to my stomach this morning."

"That's because you're hungry," I said, and under the weight of her glance I was suddenly anxious and uneasy.

"No. It's been like this all through this summer. Things sticking and me being sick. I keep thinking about everything, and the way everything's changing. Even at night. In the dark. When the others are talking, I'm thinking."

"But you never used to think," I said.

"No, but I do now."

"What about?"

"Everything. That factory, mostly. An then about everything else that comes into my mind. An in the dark, everything's different. In the dark, that factory doesn't seem so manageable. An the people in it: they don't seem so thorough in the dark—just kinda skinny an bet an lonesome. Lonesome an bet, like them little Protestant widder women in them houses out at Herbert Park. An I think about them, an then the factory, an I could cry. I told Alice, but she said that's because me bladder's near me eyes."

"But you never cry," I said.

"No, I know, but I could now, about everything. Maybe I'm grown peculiar."

"Or crazy," I said. "An for God's sake, what'll they say when they know you've quit your job?"

"Who cares?" she replied—but just the same, from the look she threw me, doubt I knew was flowing.

"It was three shillings a week," I reminded her, and thought the loss of that might well be something to cry about. And then I remembered Mrs. Murphy and her threat. "An your mother. What'll you tell her?"

"Nothing," she said swiftly, "because she won't know." She eyed me straight. "An you won't tell her. You'll call for me every morning, like you always do. Understand?"

"But what about Saturday, and her three shillings?" I asked.

"I have a plan," she said, and paused. "In future, I'm selling the best of the cinders." She swiped at her hair, shiny black, sometimes cut by me, but mostly—in a temper—by herself. "All I have to do is sell three sacks at a bob a sack to make what oul Nolan was paying me."

"But why give up the milk?" I asked.

"Because I want more time to collect the cinders, to make the money I'll need to begin dealing with," she said, and I knew then that this plan, unlike all the others, was something she had given time and long thought to.

And then: "Remember Florrie Conners?" she asked.

I nodded.

"So what did Florrie do?"

"Quit skivvying for the Jews on the South Circular, got a lend off wan a them and went to London an became a hoor."

"Exactly," Annie grinned. "Well, there's this connection," she said.

I couldn't see one. I remembered Florrie and her

escape from the street and the soured tenements. I remembered the news without malice or platitude drifting up and being gone over like fingers through hair in search of lice by every man, woman, and child in the street. I remembered Mrs. Murphy telling me Florrie was gone. "To snowy sheets," Mrs. Murphy said, "and the flaunting gorgeousness of silk and satin." And then, later, the men round the mouth of the lane talking about the gaudy blossom Florrie was, and in the street's favored crannies, the fellas fisting pricks through trouser pockets, while the shattered, like Nan Oxer, the ex-nun, flattened lips or plundered hope and said fuck all. But try as I might, I could see no connection between what Florrie had done and Annie's decision to give up the milk round.

"That's only because you don't have Barker's biscuit factory staring you in the face," Annie said. "But I do. An apart from what me Ma had to say for herself this morning, it's time I did something quick if I'm to stay outa that factory." She paused and, throwing a critical, slanted look at me, added, "An in all truth, it's time you did something. I mean," she said, seeing some explanation was necessary, "I know they won't take on youngfellas your age in Barker's but if you quit Cribbens, then we could both start dealing in September."

"But who wants to be a dealer?" I asked.

"I do," Annie replied, "because that way I can still stay on the streets and earn my living."

"But we'd need a cart," I said.

"I'm getting a cart," Annie replied. "I'm getting Ellen Simms' cart. Ellen Simms is giving up dealing the end of August and she's giving me her cart—and her customers, if I want them. Ellen Simms said I'd make a very good dealer. An I think you would, too, if you tried."

"But I don't want to be a dealer," I said.

"Why not?"

"Because I don't," I said.

"What do you want?"

"I don't know." But I did. I longed for the permanent in people and things and places; and just lately I'd found myself wanting the long past to stay. What I didn't want was to quit Cribbens. My job with him was safe. He gave me two shillings a week, and . . .

"—An when the humor's on him, as much damaged fruit as you can carry," Annie mocked. "An on top a that, you have to put up with his wife and his slob of a son, and stand to attention when he's drunk, and sing 'God Save the Queen.' "

"Only on a Saturday," I said, "an the work itself is only two to three hours a day."

"It's no such thing," Annie said quickly. "It's eight on Saturday, and don't forget he gets two of us for that lousy two bob, for many is the Saturday I have to help you."

"Only in the winter, and only with the coal."

"Even so, Cribbens is still a robber."

"But, two shillings," I said, for many was the Saturday the two shillings I earned had to keep our house in food till Monday. And then just suppose Ellen Simms didn't quit dealing and didn't give Annie her cart? And in the meantime, where was my two shillings a week to come from?

"Important questions all," Annie said, but there was no great hurry on her to answer them, for she had halted to look up at the shrouded windows of Miz Robey's hoorhouse. Smart as a whip, she ran up the steps to the hall door, gave the jazzy, free-making knock some of Miz Robey's gentlemen callers gave, then darted back to where I was standing.

"You can make that glittering two shillings on the cinders," she said. "An another thing—Ellen Simms never breaks a promise."

"How do you know, when she's never made you one?"
I asked, troubled at this swift turn in the tide of my affairs,
which, like the morning and this summer, seemed to be getting out of hand.

"I just know," Annie said, her eyes riveted on the hall
door, which was being opened a cautious slit, through which
we saw, not Miz Robey, but Lepping Lena's patterned ki-
mono and yellow straw head. We saw her paint-glazed face
and heard her flung curse, and then the door was closed
again.

"What about all the promises Miz Robey's made us
and never kept?" I said as we moved on, hoping to dissuade
Annie from the course she had taken, and from the one I
knew full well I was about to take.

"Miz Robey's a liar and a robber," Annie said, and
she was grinning, the grin I loved but was wary of because
it left me with no will of my own and made me do things I
knew I shouldn't. "But Ellen Simms is neither."

"What'll I tell my mother?"

"Nothing," Annie replied, "for, like mine, she won't
know."

"That's five bob we'll have to make."

Annie nodded. "Easy," she said, and in her voice was
the supremely indifferent ring to be heard in the voices of
the dealers in Camden Street, all doing, like Balzac, their
rosary on the money theme.

Outside Wigger Quinn's sweet shop, we automatically
stopped. On the righthand corner, a piece of cardboard
patched a break in the glass. I put my hand against it and
it gave easy. Round the street, none of the others had discovered the trick of the cardboard, and Annie and I kept
the knowledge to ourselves. "It's too easy," she used to say,
and sometimes we didn't go near it for days. But that morning, we stood and savored. At least, I did, in spite of the
indefinable hold of anxiety gripping my guts.

"Nuttyers," I said, naming my choice.

"*No.*" Annie hung back. Her eyes roved suspiciously over the tray of sweets. "I'm sick of passion rousers," she said (for round the street Nutty Favorites were considered to be a mild aphrodisiac). "Besides," she went on, "if we're to make money, we should take only what we know we can sell."

"What, then?"

"Sen-Sen," she said, "the hoors' sweets. Miz Robey's girls will buy them." Pushing back the cardboard, I watched her bony hand slide in past mine. "An no colloguing behind my back, otherwise you'll be devouring the profits."

I handed back the three packets of Sen-Sen I had been holding onto—and saw her look past me into the street, still deserted in a lonely loveliness. Into it, from Ranalagh and the canal at one end, the air came cool and carried a wet freshness that buffeted the slow, searching flight of the gulls coming up from the Liffey and touching with the tips of spread wings the black glitter of smooth cobbles. In what was left of the dawn, sounds dropped and gathered and fell away, making room for the lonesome keen of a distant foghorn, like kids in a crowded bed shifting over for a late-comer; and beside me Annie sniffed, in an effort to trace the source of the nearer sound we had caught.

"It's the hoors," I said.

"Or a copper," she murmured, alert and probing with sight and sense the dark shapes that were mouths of lanes and shriveled tenements clawing space between huckster shops, struck here and there by the green pools of light coming dawny from gas lamps edging sidewalks. At the town end of the street, the moon peered sly from the folds of thunderous clouds, like a pale-faced lady's child eyeing Annie and me from behind thick curtains, and in Harecourt Street station a thick-bellied engine shunted.

"I hope it's the Fusilier," Annie said, and I knew she was starving: the Fusilier was a black-browed baker, with a high van pulled by a gray mare, and he made morning deliveries to the shops and left the door of the van open as he did so, giving us time to swipe a loaf or a clatter of buns. But whoever it was was in no hurry, and we continued to scan the distance that later in the morning would lose all suggestion of threat in the light that breaks in splinters of green and gold and luminous waves of gray on Dublin.

"I hope it's not the dead," I said, for some mornings we stumbled into the wagon taking the unknown and unwanted who had died in the city's hospitals during the night up to the Union for burying in quicklime. The sight of the wagon and the stealthy trot of the horse always upset Annie like nothing else could, and after a stunned first stare she would fling jeers and abuse up to the thin, gray, sour-faced driver and, flaring defiance, accuse him of grave-robbing and the hospitals of murdering the innocent, and then, after he had passed, hurry like crazy to do something. She would put stones into the milk urns and ladle out wrong measures and deliberately leave the saucers off jugs, so that the cats could get at it. Or she would go running to back-chat with fury a gang of hefty, singing hoors coming home in horse-drawn cabs, daring them to their faces to stop and chase us, and then wait, brazen, until some hoor like Ninety Byrne got within an inch of her before she twisted out of reach on a laugh. But this summer, she had gone further than ever before and had done anything that had suddenly occurred to her. Before, she had come to grips only with the hoors in cabs, but lately she had taken to stopping the tired, bewildered foot-sloggers, with their white faces, kohl-black eyes, and black satin coats, returning to rooms in lanes off the street, home from Stephen's Green and the grand streets off it; and halting even those we didn't know, she would give them milk to drink and watch while they drank it, and in return get from them confessions of shillings and pounds stashed in little handbags clutched to bellies. Wide-eyed and solemn, she would listen to complaints or sagas of achievement spilled out from mouths that nights and scores had pulped, and afterward, standing stiff and sickened and empty, she would say, "I just wish I could pull this whole, lousy street down."

One morning, after meeting the death wagon, she went down a lane and to everyone in it gave away the two full urns of milk free; and on another, emptied the lot into the canal at the locks and afterward forced the door of Doyle's the news agent and robbed the till. She gave the twenty-four shillings in it to Mary Mallin, in the lane, to pay her rent and buy a coat with the balance; and later that very morning, when the whole street had gathered round Mr. Doyle and his shop, she pushed her way through the crowd to commiserate with him and then, when nobody else would, went down to Lad Lane to get the police he wanted. He gave her a shilling for her trouble, which, she was quick to point out, brought her entire takings up to twenty-five.

Laughing now, I saw her gesture me to silence as suddenly, out of the dark of Galleon's Lane, a big, striding figure flashed into the dusk of light and came swiftly up the street.

"It's Ellen Simms," Annie said, and it was, big-boned and lusty-footed, on her way out to the roads to barter at the doors of the Protestants, and pushing in front of her the yellow, three-wheeled basket cart she had promised Annie.

"Quick!" Annie drew me into the dark of a passage running between two shops. "If that wan sees us," she said, "she'll swear I'm hurrying her."

"You are," I said.

"I know," she hissed, "but I don't want her to know I am, for people always act up when they know you're depending."

We stood still, then edged out to where we could see but not be seen from the street.

"Do you know something?" she said, and she was suddenly thoughtful.

And I did and I nodded, and she was right. Ellen Simms didn't look old or tired to me, either, or ready to give up dealing.

"In fact, if I was offered a lease on that wan's life, I'd take it," Annie said.

"Maybe she'll drop dead, or be run over."

"I don't want her to drop dead or be run over," Annie snapped.

"We could get Primmy Maggot's mother to put a curse on her. She'd do it for half a dollar."

"No, I don't want anything to happen to her."

"But you want her cart."

"Not that way," she said quickly. "I'll stoop for the prize, but I'm Goddammed if I'll kill for it."

"You might, if you wanted it bad enough."

"Not Ellen Simms," she replied.

Thinking then that she was lovely staying still, I remembered again Mr. Murphy and his prediction, and felt for the second time that morning a tightness in my chest, and in some queer way, a sense rather than a feeling of fear. I could not have explained it and, about to try, I saw she wasn't listening—but the feeling was like that sudden minute of fear that strikes for no reason in the dizzy green of early spring, only this was more violent, more strident, and knife sharp.

"You won't get that cart," I said. And I had spoken in spite of myself.

"And if I don't?" she asked, and paused. "I'll get another," she said suddenly. "An if I can't buy one, I'll feck one."

And I knew she would, for Annie believed that if a thing wasn't locked or nailed down and could be moved, it was anybody's property.

"We may have to," I said. "Feck one, I mean: for we'll never make in three weeks enough to buy one."

"Why not?" she asked. "With the money we make on the sweets and the cinders?"

"Because we can't depend on the sweets. The Wigger might get that glass mended today. An Maggie Hyland and Scraps have been looting our bens for the past month."

"Hyland and Scraps will loot no more bens," she said. "An if the Wigger is fool enough to do anything with that glass, she'll be wasting her money, for I'll only have to break it again. One thing sure," she said suddenly. "I'm not going into any factory!"

"I suppose," I said, "we could make a lot of money dealing."

"With a cart we could," Annie said. "Why, we could do even better than Ellen Simms," she cried, and now there was no interval in the speed of our stares. "Together, we could get through more houses than she does. Sell things she doesn't."

"What, for instance?" I asked. For Ellen Simms sold coal briquettes, house plants, fruit and vegetables, and in my mind's eye I saw the stiff cold fur of slaughtered rabbits and the shocked eyes of Friday's fish.

"Ah, stuff!" Annie exclaimed.

And then, from the mothering speed of uncertain thought, I brought her with another question.

"I don't know," she said. "We could ask." Across the street, Ellen Simms was halting in the first pause she had made up it. "Ask Ellen Simms," Annie said. "Let on you want to know for yourself."

I left the wall and the shadows hiding us and stepped into the street. I heard Ellen Simms give a grim amused chuckle and thought it no wonder that, apart from Annie and myself, everyone else round the street was afraid of her. I couldn't see her eyes, but I felt their weight. I saw her hold herself stiff in very much the way Annie sometimes held herself, and then, with a flick of her hand, I watched her smooth out the cloth flung over the top of the cart before, with a swift turn of her head, she said, "Faith, and there's nothing glittering about your progress today."

"It's early," I said. I moved toward her over the cobbles.

"You look like a gent picking his steps. Or is it thoughtful you are?" she asked.

"I was wondering."

"What about?" She questioned rough.

"The cost of a cart like yours."

"I wouldn't know."

"Didn't you buy yours?" I asked.

"No, I didn't. I was what you might call a reluctant inheritor." She let her black shawl slacken on her shoulders, and I knew that behind me, in the dark of the passage, a meditative look would be absorbing Annie's face. I also knew she would be wanting to know who Ellen Simms had inherited her cart from, and for a split second I wondered if I should ask, but decided against it.

"I was thinking of buying one," I said, and now I could see her face. And the ripple of humor she shoved aside from her mouth rose to the caverned brown eyes.

"You look as if you could afford to," she said, and I was glad she noticed my hat and coat, for she liked to see you in the things she gave.

"I'm serious, but . . . ," I said.

"You'd have to be at this hour of the morning," she replied, and I thought she looked past me to the passage where Annie was hiding, but I couldn't be sure, for the action of the glance was too swift. "You know I'm giving that other anarchist this one," she said. "But you'd like to know what they cost in case I don't, is that it?" she asked, and without waiting for an answer: "Well, I'll find out and let youse know."

"When?" I asked.

"Today or tomorrow." Her glance went from me to the bridge and, beyond it, to the misty, rising folds of the Dublin mountains and the big, udder-swinging clouds mitering them. She withdrew her gaze. "Can youse wait that long?" she asked, and the smile she threw me was a rare one.

"We'll have to," I said, and I saw her mouth, that even now quivered with fighting perseverance, curve upward. She folded herself back into the armor of her shawl, clasped again the handle of her cart and, without another word, headed for the bridge.

"Did she have her pipe with her?" Annie asked as we watched Ellen Simms go straight-backed into the shrinking dusk and, at the bridge, pause just before she took it.

"In the pocket of her apron," I said, and knew there was no need for me to repeat what Ellen Simms had said, for Annie had heard every word.

"Come on," she said and, pulling my arm, turned me in the direction of the street and the road at the end, that would take us to the squares and the basements of the houses where the bens were kept.

3

In Fitzwilliam Square, leftover rain from the night before made small pools on the slabbed sidewalks. In the park in the center, purple butterfly bush plumes tossed in heavy plenty under snowy whimples of Indian bean, and from flaunting drifts of copper-barked rowans, crimson berries fell and were lost in the warm smell of long grass greening the space between railings and locked gates.

Outside houses high and mighty, with delicate fanlights, stately doors, and flashing windows, servants in blue and pink dresses, starched aprons, and white caps polished brass plates, letter-box flaps, and heavy knockers of bronze and brass. In the gutter on the Pembrooke Street side of the square, Jesus, as if in subtle sympathy with the wind plucking fitful at the trees' blossoms, played an air of his own on a tin whistle; and from the lane that led to St. Vincent's Hospital, the school, and the dead house, Brennan the

Builder came, venting his foam-lipped laugh that rippled a shudder along the walls of the lane behind him.

From the yawns of basements, cinder-pickers darted, the young and sturdy going at the double, while behind them, with backs bent from hunger and the weight of sacks, the clumsy and thick-headed streeled, backhanding eyes heavy with sleep; and, behind these, the crippled limped, nagged on by the timid and infirm, who whinged and scavenged in their tracks. Through them all, like threads in a tapestry, the sly snarled a way, and the crafty, who had made themselves known to servants and cooks, paused sudden to barter a find or swap a bowl of dripping or a loaf of bread; while others, with dust-gray faces and open mouths, slowed to scratch or stare furtive at roughs who were not cinder-pickers but thieves, with the feet of lumberjacks.

Kids we knew, like the Kelly twins and Jim Mac and his sister Carmel, sat on the path to gnaw a meatbone or a handful of meat scraps, while others pocketed with care a bit of sugar or a few grains of tea, elbowed by lushes who, still touched by gaiety, guzzled quick slugs from bottles, port that streamed purple.

Above them, Bessie the Pig strode and behind her, but at a distance, Lady Hamilton, followed by four youngfellas who walked in a constant trot in his wake, and spoke to nobody. They were the same height as Annie and me and, we guessed, the same age, but who they were or where they came from nobody knew, and Lady Hamilton himself never said. They had shaven heads and red knitted mufflers they buried them in, and from the back they looked as if their heads had been cut off. Annie said they were good robbers, but they looked lifeless and grinned stony, but only at Annie, and left the firm grip Lady Hamilton kept on them to do so. Unhindered they went, like us, but never strayed, as we did, to look at a sight that dared the wandering eye, or paused to back-chat the brazen the way Annie did, or question the way she would the sudden affluence of another. Unlike us, they sidestepped as in a reel the troublesome, those men and women who begged the price of a bottle and then, in short and gallant hours, sang out or cried sudden or flung a curse onto the flippant air at us or at the young roughs, like Johnny Roscoe, chatting up some thick of a servant, while behind their backs he threw a lewd gesture at a mocking milkman or somber-suited postman.

They saw, as we did, Aggie the Saint streeling noisy and stout-bellied, endorsing the morning and the paupers crowding it, but shied from her; and the quiet women who, hatted and coated, went with clean faces and soda-raw hands from door to door, braving the muttered-in-passing obscenities of the cinder-pickers and the insolent rebuffs of culchi servants, in desperate search of a day's scrubbing or a week's washing.

"Work that even if they get they won't be paid for," Annie said that morning as we watched, and she eyed moody a frail, white-haired woman walking away from the door of the house, and the basement into which we were about to descend. "A mean house," Annie said. "An a mean, lousy half-dollar is all they pay for a full day's scrubbing. The people who own this house should be jailed," she said, shouting her trumpet-tongued resistance to wrong up to the bull of a servant slamming the door in our faces. "You'd think that wan could've found something for that woman to do," she cried. "Or, if not, at least given her something to eat." She paused and glared up at the massive doorway, placid and dark with obedience. "This must be one of the meanest kips in Dublin. I've a good mind to belt hell outa that door and tell that skivvie what I think of her."

"She knows," I said. "For, don't you remember, you told her last week? An the week before that?"

"Well, I'll tell her again this week, for she seems to have forgotten."

"They can't give work to every woman who knocks," I said.

"Maybe not," Annie replied. "But that culchi's not even mannered with people. She could tell them nice, that wouldn't cost her anything, would it?"

"She'll stop us doing the bens, if you're not careful," I warned, uneasy at the strength and carrying power of Annie's voice when she was angry.

"Let her try," she cried. "What that beef-heeled culchi needs is a couple of good bricks through them windows."

"What she needs, pet, you haven't got." Mollo Ross paused on her way from the basement we were standing at to the one next door. "But Johnny Roscoe has," she said on a laugh that took her on.

Annie stared after her. "What's that wan talking about?" she asked, and with her glance puzzled and fixed on me, didn't see Scraps coming till he was beside us.

"Ah, Jasus," he cried. "Don't tell us you haven't done this kip yet?"

Annie swung round, then tensed, the way the gulls did when they went against the wind to cut it sideways.

"Oh, it's you," she snapped, and her eyes, wide apart, were as dark as beer held to light.

"Who did you think it was?" Scraps bent in cantankerous complaint.

"Daddy Christmas," Annie said, and swung her sack in a wide, arrogant sweep from shoulder to shoulder.

"Oh, very funny." Scraps, tittering, shuffled forward. "But enough of the gas and the smart quips, for unless you intend turning the square into a garden of repose, might I suggest you get on with them bens?"

"I will, of course," Annie said, and above her the dull rheumy eyes, screwed up against the wind, latched on to her face.

"But, right now," she said, "there's no great hurry on me."

"Maybe not," Scraps cried. "But I can't mitch round here all day. I've other things to do."

"What kinda things?" Annie asked, sounding interested.

"That's my business," Scraps replied.

"An the bens are ours," Annie said. "We'll do them when we're ready."

"Not if I have any say in the matter."

"You haven't." Annie looked him over. "These happen to be our bens," she said, and she spoke slow and held herself stiff, but ready to duck if she had to.

"Come on," I said, and through the clash of their glances I suddenly moved. Annie followed, but only after a long backward look at him as she came through the gate to the steps that led down to the basement.

"Thieving, shagging rabble-rousers," Scraps muttered, and then, behind us, began to air old grievances.

"We don't have to let him near our bens," Annie said loud. And she was right, but he had been doing them after us for as long as I could remember, and now there was no way of stopping him. Long and gray he was, and thin, with a pointed nose that was never dry, and loose, gray skin that matched in color eyes you wanted to shelter from. He wore a battered gray felt on his gray head, and a gray-blue overcoat that streeled. He carried a sack for the cinders and a pillow-slip for wrap-ups and a black stumpy stick he ran up youngwans' dresses. He lived near us, in Rock Street, with his wife, a silent, buxom hoor who hustled in broad daylight the dark paths of Stephen's Green and the banks of the canal, but mostly the canal. She walked upright and proud, but he was a go-be-the-wall who got from servants and cooks who hadn't the courage to even open doors to Annie and me. He was afraid of Annie, and he disliked her, and skirted round her with caution, always. She didn't like him, either, and knew that he and Maggie Hyland rifled our bens some mornings before we got to them, and shared the proceeds among themselves. "One a these days, we'll catch Scraps and Maggie Hyland," Annie said, but we never did.

Now, glancing at him, Annie said, "You an Hyland will have to find your own bens." She threw her sack to the ground and whipped the lid off the first of the three bens.

"Oh, yes?" Scraps raised brows that blossomed mean over narrow eyes.

"Yes," Annie said. "For from now on, we'll be taking every single cinder we can carry."

"You always do," Scraps muttered, and continued to utter complaints against us which we pretended not to hear.

He was watching Annie, but there was no pause in her rise and fall over the ben as she extracted with speed the good black cinders from the gray and the gray from the clinkers that came from coke and were veined with orange. These were useless and she threw them aside and dropped the cinders that came from coal into the mouth of the sack held up and open in her left hand.

"That culchi's not only mean, but dirty," she complained suddenly. "Look." She held up a handful of cinders. "This wan's mixing these with the slops just for spite."

"You should tell her off," Scraps said.

"I told her off," Annie replied.

And she had. Last week and the week before—and not in any chancing way, either. Twice she had gone storming up to the massive hall door, because the thick of a servant, out of the west and with hardly a word of English, wouldn't open the kitchen door to us.

"An what did she say?" Scraps asked.

Annie glanced at him. "Nothing," she said, "for, like you, she seemed to be hard a hearing."

"Maybe she didn't understand. These countrywans can be terrible dense. You'd have to explain to her."

"I did," Annie said, and she had, in detail, how all the other servants in the squares kept the cinder bens separate from the bens holding only slops; and the servant had listened, her heavy face impassive, sullen, her stupid eyes moseying in half wonder from my hat and coat to Annie's bare feet and cropped head, before she withdrew suddenly and slammed the door in our faces.

"It was always a poverty-stricken house, this wan," Scraps said, and left the support the wall was to peer in through the big, wide-curtained window behind us. "There's never a thing a man could help himself to. But then this pack are Romans, so what can youse expect?"

"Nothing." Annie, on a change of mood and nearing the end of the first ben, paused to speak and to watch him, before she began, with me, to explore mine.

"Good Protestant bens are what you need, Scraps," she said, and she was out now to provoke, for she knew the use of the nickname would vex.

"An that's what I had, till our own lot of misbegotten savages took over," Scraps muttered. "An, with the help of God, good Protestant bens are what we'll have again."

"You can't be looking," Annie told him. "For there's still a few black Protestants holding out in Leeson Street. Try Leeson Street."

"Well, you know . . . ," he began, and he was suddenly thoughtful. "I just might, 'cept a course I'm hampered by shyness an afraid of making a show of meself be making a move at which I did badly. No, on second thoughts, I'll stay where I am," he said, and he left the window and, after trying the latch on the door of the kitchen, went back to stand at the wall.

"You won't shift him," I muttered to Annie.

"Will youse be long?" he asked, but we didn't answer. "I remember," he said, "when a man on his tod couldn't carry the weight of the stuff these houses threw out. Boulders of coal, and suits, and clawhammer coats that never felt the scorch of a back. . . ."

"Not to mention the wrap-ups the cooks and footmen threw youse," Annie cut in, to slice short the litany he was about to embark on. "Well, times have changed, buster," she said, irritating him with the slur of mockery roughing her voice, that brushed aside all attempts he was making to ingratiate. "In fact, any day now you and a few others I know are going to have to try your hands at a day's work, an you won't like that, either."

He stooped and pounced suddenly on a cinder that fell from my hand and threw it into his own sack.

"I've a good mind to take that back," Annie muttered. And before she would've, but all she did that morning was throw him a look he caught and grinned at as he left the wall and shuffled over to the bens.

"We haven't finished yet," I said.

"But youse are down to the ashes." He was all surprise. "Ah, Jasus," he cried sudden, and drew back. "What are youse trying to do? Defraud me?"

"We wouldn't dream of it," Annie laughed, and Scraps jumped, or I thought he did. His feet left the ground, and for a second he seemed to soar, and the ends of his coat billowed and flapped in the cold wind that always chilled to freezing the gapes of the basements.

"You'll take off if you're not careful," Annie laughed into his face. "Try a reel," she suggested, and the street above us, distracted by the sounds he was making, paused to look down, then went away.

Scraps pointed. "Youse are down to the shagging ashes." He looked bewildered. "Ah, now," he said, and his mouth trembled. "For Christ's sake." He pushed me aside, his mouth twisting into strange shapes as Annie straightened up to face him.

"What are youse leaving us?" he asked.

"I don't have to leave you anything," Annie replied, and from the battering-ram of her stare he backed down.

"Leave us enough to put under a kettle," he begged, desperate.

"Why?" Annie asked, in the stubborn, questioning mood that vexed saints.

"Because you always do." Scraps swung himself out and stood sideways.

"But I don't have to," Annie said, and between them the silence was suddenly heavy and thick.

"All right—you don't have to," he said, and Annie nodded.

"Okay, as long as you know," she said, and added: "An, while we're at it, from this morning on, we don't aim to leave nothing in our bens."

"I don't know in the name a Jasus what's come over you, for your mood is suddenly anything but giving."

"I don't have to give you anything," Annie said.

"So you don't—but be reasonable," he cried. "Sure, don't I always do the bens after youse?"

"So do a whole lot of others," Annie said, "but that doesn't mean we have to rob ourselves for you *or* them."

"All right, I won't fight you," he said softly, and then

a shout came into his voice. "Only don't come the boss lady
with me. What you're leaving in them bens won't be worth
bending me back for." And now there was a roar in the
voice, seldom raised on the squares, and with his attention
and sight riveted on Annie, who had to strain her neck back
to look up at him, he didn't see Bessie the Pig come to the
railings overhead and fling herself against them.

"In that case, mister, an in your particular circumstances, you shouldn't exert yourself," Bessie roared and,
laughing, flung her sack to the ground. One hand on her bad
hip, she clutched for support the spike of the railing with
the other. "Like the Little Flower, I'm always where I'm
needed," she said gaily, her smile big as she shook from her
face the wild, red hair which was neither pinned nor tied and
which lashed crimson the motley dome of sky above her.

"Not this time," Scraps said up to her.

"What's a go-be-the-wall after?" Bessie, ignoring him,
looked down into Annie's raised face.

"The best of our bens." Annie had to squint to see in
the sharp light shadowing Bessie.

"An you'll give him them," Bessie said. "For he surely
is a remarkable soul, and his presence down there must be
a great encouragement to youse. After all, it isn't every day
you come across a hoormaster chiseling childer out of a few
lousy cinders."

"I'm chiseling nothing." Scraps glared up at her.

"Now that's a lie," Bessie said. "A red an roaring lie.
For with me own ears I heard you ranting an raving a mile
away. In fact, I was just about to bid the time a day with
Aggie the Saint on her way to pray for the Pope's intentions
and an early diddly, when me ears were smote with your
venom."

"What's that?" I asked.

"An Aggie said, 'Slaughter, Ma'am, down among the moon daisies,' before she hurried off, drunk on the blood a martyrs, an left me to go through the formularies of getting here alone, an just in time, if I'm any judge of the apple-cheeked in tantrums."

"Ah, fuck off," Scraps yelled, and the laugh lingering on Bessie's face was wiped clean.

"You dirty-tongued oul bastard," she cried, and the voice, that had been deep, dark, and husky, became a roar that could be heard all over the square. "Ya filth," she yelled, and aimed a spit of disgust down at him. "Denying everybody but yourself an your scarlet hoor a Babylon the right to live."

"I'm denying nobody nothing!" Scraps screamed. "I'm minding me own business, which is what you should be doing, you moithering oul ox."

"I'll give you five seconds to jubilate yourself up outa there," Bessie said. "After that, I'll climb down them steps an devour ya."

"You an what shagging army?"

"I'll lift you," Bessie yelled, "from your rambling caution, you hoormonger, if you ever raise a hand to them childer again."

Scraps vented a laugh. "Be Jasus, an they're the right childer," he sneered. "It's a long time since this pair a sharks keened over the milky white of a fat diddy. Why, there isn't a house between here an Blackrock that'll open its doors to either of them."

"No, but they open them wide for you," Bessie roared. "You trollop—think I don't know what your game is, with your little black stick?" She paused and bent suddenly and fished out from the pockets of one of her skirts a twist of paper, opened it carefully and, between thumb and forefinger, took a pinch of snuff. "Come on," she cried, "I'm waiting," and then, with great care, held the fingers with the snuff in them tight up to each nostril and sniffed hard.

"You'll wait," Scraps yelled. "That's all she's good for," he muttered. "Snuff, an tempting any oul fool an Saint-hunter she comes across to part with their pennies. Stuffed, them skirts are, with novenas an medals she cadges round the convents, then peddles round the Pillar an up in that kip of a room she has behind the Four Courts."

"I'll stuff you," Bessie said. "An it won't be with medals or novenas. I'll leave you soft enough for hoors to lean on."

"You'll have to exert yourself, then." Scraps, brave with the knowledge that her size and hip made the flight of steps down to the basement an obstacle not even Bessie could overcome, tittered up at her; then, bending double, he went to the foot of the steps and, for a second, looked as if he were about to charge up them. But he didn't. Instead, scuffling into a dance, he filled the air round us with an obscene chant.

"I'll get ya!" Bessie roared, and reared to her full height, while I went to the window of the kitchen behind us.

"She'll bring that culchi out," I said, but the kitchen was empty, except for the cook, who was deaf and stood with her back to the window, at a sink stacked with delph.

"I'll get ya," Bessie screamed, "the minute you set foot up here."

"I hope it keeps fine for you." Scraps had come to the end of his chant. "Be Jasus," he said suddenly, "I'm nicely hoped up, for if I'm not robbing kids, I'm raping them."

"If you're doing neither, what are you doing down there?" Bessie was suddenly calmer than she had been.

"Watching over us," Annie laughed. "He's afraid we'll come to some harm."

"I'm minding me own business," Scraps said.

Bessie laughed. "Of course. Your scattered interests would need minding." Looking from him, and in a sudden change of mood, she said, "Far be it from me to impose any of me own notions on another, but if I was youse, I wouldn't turn me back on that thing, for he'd think nothing of knifing you."

"He'd want to be outa his mind to chance anything on us," Annie said, but her glance, shifting from Bessie to Scraps, was wary and watchful.

"He is," Bessie said. "For, like Brennan the Builder, it's only a matter of time before they seal the pair a them up for ever, with all their tormenting delusions." She paused. "Sure, there isn't a herb in the world that could heal that man's wounds. An look," she said, "at them rheumy oul eyes. Sure, you've only to cast your lovely wans on them to see that neither man nor beast is safe beside him."

He stared in front of him and, above us, Bessie suddenly sat down and began, after a pause, to count the pennies she had begged and gathered in her streel across the town that morning, and to murmur at the top of her voice a constant stream of thoughts, some of which she meant for us and the rest for anyone who cared to listen.

"One a these mornings, she'll bring them spendthrifts of energy down on us," Scraps said, and he meant the police.

"All the more reason for you to push off," Annie said, eyeing him strangely before she stooped again over the bens. And I knew then that what Bessie had said was soaking her mind with uneasiness. "Be terrible if he was mad," she whispered. "Specially when you think a the hard time I give him."

"He doesn't look mad," I said.

"Maybe not," Annie replied. "But it doesn't always show: what about Mary Doyle."

"Just the same . . . ," I began, but just then Bessie

screamed and Scraps cried, "Oh, good Jesus," and Annie and I straightened up.

"A pox on youse," Bessie roared. "A pox on the lot a youse."

"What happened?" Annie cried. "What's up?"

"Duped!" Bessie shrieked. "Look at this." She pushed her hand through the railings. "A bad penny," she cried, "a bad, shagging penny."

Annie took the penny. "It's a copper medal," she said, and passed it on to me and I handed it back to Bessie. She took it and then yelled at a passerby.

"C'm're, Ma'am, an if this isn't as crooked as that thing below in the basement, inform me what is."

There was a pause, a mumbling of words, and then Bessie said, "Oh, Jasus, aren't they desperate but the ponces, lousers, and thieves a decent person has to consort with?"

"Terrible," Annie said, and the laugh she couldn't hold back interrupted the lament Bessie was now lathering the morning with.

"Ah, no, Annie." Bessie's reproach was loud and plaintive and injured. "If that wouldn't put a blush on the yellowing dead of a nun's kisser, what would?"

"Who do you think gave it to you?" Annie threw me a grin.

"Some dirty, perjured animal," Bessie said. "Put it into me hand when me poor, disheveled mind was elsewhere. Some schemer, catching sight of what's left of me innocence before ruthless hands mauled it to prevent me becoming the lovely occasion for sin I was—fingered it, he did, from the assortment of coins straining the lining of his pockets—an, big a heart, thought he'd plunder the nest-egg."

"Some comic," Annie said.

"Or hoormaster," Bessie replied. "On his way to early

Mass, caught sight of me as I crossed under the Pillar or took shelter from that last shower under the dome a the Four Courts, an said to hisself, 'I'll unbalance the margin a that wan's mind today, that's what I'll do.' "

"A slip, maybe?" Annie supposed, but on a burst of impatience, Bessie dismissed supposition scornfully.

"Sorra a slip," she cried. "This was done to desecrate me own sad disorder with further dishonor. This was done for spite. The bad penny well placed—the lousy penny took in badness from its ceaseless spin by some rotten hand and passed into mine. As if I hadn't plucked enough bitter wisdom from the streets an kitchens of this town already."

"Give it to wan of the shops," Annie said, slowed up by the hint of a cry that had crept into the voice above us. "If you leave it till evening, they wouldn't see it in the dark."

"Give it to the chapel man," Scraps said, but Bessie ignored him:

"A bad penny, child a grace, threw to placate me own offended heart."

"Jasus, what would she do if it was a bad pound-note?"

"Nobody," Annie told Scraps, "is talking to you." And above us, Bessie gave vent to sudden anger.

"The curse a God on that long-spined man who waltzed by. Buying hisself, by a lousy trick, the luxury of a laugh."

"It wouldn't have bought him the mansion house," Scraps tittered foolishly.

"He'll rear in grief, that man," Bessie said, "an sizzle in poxy delirium in a hen-house, an that he may, for the gray of the stone sheltering the troubled would be more than he deserves. I remember him now!" she cried sudden. "Like that ferret down there beside youse, this was another with a bent mind. Another vomit, maybe, with a hoor of a wife scything the grass of the canal with legs in white silk stockings. Another hoor with her legs spread apart, an not in boistrous dance, either, but shaped to succour the randy and rigid between her fat, sleek knees."

"Ah—put a sock in it, for fuck's sake," Scraps roared up at the face that was now turned sideways.

"It's the truth," Bessie said, and gazed stupid at nothing.

"Ah, shut up," Scraps cried.

"You leave her alone," Annie hissed, and I gathered up the pile of black cinders she had, as always, set aside for Bessie.

"She's a troublemaker," Scraps yelled, and the spit foaming his mouth fell in a shower between himself and Annie.

Annie drew the back of her hand across her face, and over it her eyes flashed in fight. "She's not the only one," she said. "An another thing, you've no right to come down them steps till we've gone up them."

"It's what the others all do," I added.

"I'm not interested in what the others all do," Scraps mimicked me. "An any more guff outa you an you'll feel the weight a me hand across your gob."

"An we'd let you," Annie said, and between Scraps and me she bent and hoisted her sack up on to her back.

"Have youse left me anything?" he asked, going to where the bens were.

"Why don't you look?" Annie spoke from the steps, but I knew she had—for, apart from the cinders she had set aside for Bessie, she had, when she thought my attention was elsewhere, set aside in one of the bens a stack of black cinders for him.

"The treacherous, conniving oul bastard," Bessie said as I put her share of the cinders in the sack at her feet. She drew the sack closer to her skirts. "Bands a robbers," she

said, scanning the path and the people on it. "An not a
policeman within bugle-call a this place if you was been
murdered. Where do they get to?" she asked suddenly.

"Who?" Annie asked.

"Ah, the policemen." Bessie stared hard at Annie.
"A woman could be scattered, mangled, battered an bet, an
the cinders stole right under her eyes, without wan a them
showing a face to even puzzle this lot in their pilfering."
Her glance, rowdy and rampant, swept the square. She got
to her feet, and her greeny eyes stared in front of her.
"Wait now," she said, and limped quick out into the middle
of it.

"For what?" I asked. But Annie didn't answer. She
was looking past me to where Brennan the Builder, frothing
Irish at Biddser Mulvey, who didn't understand a word of
it, stood, watched by a servant on the steps above them.
New to the square, the servant had left the hall door wide
open.

"Now, if we could get into that hall," Annie said
quietly.

"Let's try," I said.

Annie grinned. "Only go slow," she whispered.

And we did, but the servant saw us and, after a quick
stare, slammed the hall door behind her. Biddser Mulvey,
searching for the cause, saw us and laughed.

"Jasus," she said, "youse are great at clearing the place
of invaders. People have only to see youse coming to put
themselves and their possessions under lock and key. That
girl turned white at the sight a youse."

"Pity about her." Annie drew alongside Biddser.

"Anyway, that hall is empty," Biddser said. "There
wasn't even an umbrella in it. An as for that skivvie, she'd
a been no use to youse, for it was here her interest lay."
Wiry and bright, she tossed her head toward Brennan.

"Did she give him anything?" Annie asked.

"A scapular." Biddser gazed up at Brennan, who stood stonily grinning and chanting breathless the bits of Irish he had stumbled on. "Show them," she said, but Brennan wouldn't.

"It doesn't matter," Annie said, her restless glance on the go for something that did, and then finding it as, up from a basement a few yards away, Maggie Hyland came, lugging behind her a sack half full of what we knew would be good black cinders. I heard a sharp intake of breath, and the next minute Annie had jumped distance; and, backed up against the railings, Maggie Hyland was making squeals of unmerciful fright.

4

Maggie Hyland was a
beggar who ran with beggars. She liked youngfellas and
spoke to them sweet and acted sly. She kept herself clean
and neat with resentment, her heart low, and being mean,
living a secret. Unlike Annie, who was bony and agile, Maggie Hyland was clumsy and, in spite of the dancing she took
once a week from Dolly Flynn below in the pool hall at the
bottom of Rock Street, heavy-footed. Our age, she lived in
the street and, like us, did the bens in the morning—but
unlike us, she begged soup and bread round the convents in
the afternoon. She wore shoes that were hornpipe and black
patent leather, and on Sundays knee-high stockings and pinnies that were white and gophered and lace-edged round the
neck and hem. She walked in a hippy, sexy way, and knew
things we didn't.

She knew where attendance at churches, chapels, and
prayer meetings was rewarded by coal tickets, blankets, and
boots, and knew where and when to go, and what to say.

She knew the gullible, the soft and the green, who could by tears be bamboozled for shillings, cajoled for pounds. She knew about the free dinners the nuns gave out in the Cancer Hospital on the Northbrook Road, and, in proper, wistful misery, went for them and ate them. She knew about the parties given once a year in the various dispensaries scattered throughout the city and, whereas we never did, she always had tickets for them, and for the Sunday excursions the Protestants ran out to the Scalp in the summer. Although she was a Catholic, she dug, like most beggars, with both feet—and, playing the earnest inquirer the Protestants loved, went to the Sunday school run by them in a room at the back of the church on the Adelaide Road, and imagined nobody but herself knew about it.

But we knew, because in a turbulent fit of wanting to know we followed her one Sunday, and afterward, thinking she had to, she tried to bribe us to silence with a twopence colored, of a man she claimed was the living Christ. Annie, who couldn't bend the knee, and treated those who did with tolerant indifference, wanted to know where he lived, this man whose picture she was considering with suspicion, for she thought—and so did I—that he might be another profitable sentimentalist who dabbled in the street's affairs on his own account, or administered relief for a mission, or disbursed a mansion house fund.

"Why, he lives everywhere," Maggie Hyland said. "Only you can't see him."

"In that case, how do you know where he lives?" Annie asked.

"I don't," Maggie Hyland replied. "But the woman who does the teaching says he's everywhere. And," she added, "his father has many houses."

"That's something I just don't believe," Annie told

her flatly. "To begin with, why should one man have two houses?"

"Lots of men have two houses," Maggie Hyland said.

But Annie, in one of her practical turns of mind, wanted to know how one man could live in two places at the same time. "Tell us that," she asked, and waited.

But Maggie Hyland couldn't. Then Annie said the man was an invention, and a black Protestant invention at that—for, search as she might, she could find no resemblance between the man in the picture and the white-robed, bearded benevolence in the brown frame hanging on the wall over my mother's bed.

"I'm not convinced," she told Maggie Hyland. Any more than she was convinced now by Hyland's whinged assurances that she hadn't plundered our bens, while all the time her sharp and greedy eyes darted panic for breaks she could escape through.

"In that case, you've nothing to worry about," Annie said. "But, till we've seen for ourselves, I'm holding on to this."

She tore the sack from the grip Hyland had on it, and toward Maggie's blubber sounds of fright people came running.

"Rip her up," a fella said, and a woman passing, eyeing Annie, paused to intervene, but moved on when Biddser Mulvey, abandoning Brennan, plunged into the uproar. She glared at the woman.

"Any interference from you, Ma'am, an I'll demolish you," Biddser cried. And the woman, about to speak, changed her mind and moved on.

"Your spine should be bent," Biddser said and, baring her teeth like a cat, stuck her face close in to Maggie Hyland's. "You're not even a cinder-picker," she said quickly.

"You're a scavenger and a beggar. Kicked decent is what you should be."

"An will," Annie threatened.

"We're depending on them cinders," I said.

"Even if youse weren't," Biddser glared at Maggie Hyland, "why pick on Annie's bens?" For she knew, and so did the others on the square, that Annie, when asked, and even without being asked, was generous with the cinders and anything else she got from the bens or took from round the doors. They also knew it was Annie who looked out for the maimed in mind and limb, and that she gave to Jesus and the others like him, taking desperate chances to feck the cigarettes they had to have; and that it was Annie who put the boots on their feet and kept the coats on their backs; and that it was she who scoured the streets in the depths of winter to get the eightpence that bought the beds in the night shelters.

But that viz-a-viz was neither here nor there, Biddser said. Thing was, Maggie Hyland knew shagging well she had no right to loot bens, Annie's or anybody else's, and the life should be danced out of her, and right now.

"But that's force," Brennan the Builder protested. He edged sideways between Annie and Biddser, who, when the mood was on her, shacked up with him.

"Ah, force, me balls," Biddser cried.

"Self-preservation is nature's first law," Brennan said solemnly. "Thing is for each and every one of us to find and develop our own sources." He grinned and, catching Biddser's left breast in his hand, squeezed it.

"Ah, for Christ's sake, push off, Abi." Biddser swept him aside with raddled impatience.

"Children," Brennan said, "should be taught." He looked at Biddser as if he wanted to fondle her.

"What childer?" Biddser asked.

"Them childer," Brennan pointed.

Biddser stared, like a child prematurely aware. "When have they had time to be childer?" she asked. But Brennan, stepping back, raised his eyes and suddenly thoughtless face up to the sky.

"C'm're." Biddser was looking at Annie. "Are them your cinders?"

"They're not," Maggie Hyland screamed.

"I'll find out," Annie said, and together we dived down into the basement. "They are." Annie ran her hand through the dust and clinkers that was all that was left in the two bens.

"The pauper," I said, speaking into a scream while Annie tore the cap from her head, and then, under the thin shelter of her red pinny, I could see the twin points of her breasts rise and fall.

"We'll have to do Hyland," she said and looked, for a second, the way women did when they faced each other in a fight. "Come on," she said.

But at the top of the steps, Biddser and Brennan stood alone. Biddser was frantic. "Let me glance stray for a minute, and the whippet took off," she cried. Her mouth twitched.

Annie's eyes swept the square in a wild glance, then swooped back to light on Biddser. "That's all right," she said, and she was suddenly calm.

"What d'you mean?" Biddser, flushed and agitated, stared bewildered. "You're not letting her away with it?"

Annie flicked an uncertain glance at me. "No," she said, but I knew the thought of doing so had crossed her mind. I also knew Hyland, on her own and without backing, was a poor fighter, and that in conflict Annie preferred the brave and the brazen.

But on the squares, only the short on brains and the mean, like Scraps, took from bens that were not theirs. And

even they didn't always escape. And neither did the old, who
sometimes pillaged with a clumsy affectation of absent-mind-
edness; for many a morning's flight was stunned with their
screams and the thud of blows and the crunch of fists and,
in a sudden pause, up from the depths of a basement the
angry, doleful crying of the guilty could be heard.

"Well, if youse do let her away with it, you may as well
find yourself a ferny place to hustle, for there'll be no living
for you on the squares," Biddser Mulvey said. And she was
right, for to stay on them, it wasn't enough to fight—you
had to be seen fighting.

"An what about the factory?" I asked. "An the money
you'll need to stay out of it?"

"So all right," Annie snapped, and Biddser, having—
as she thought—brought her from one mood to another,
pushed off, just as Jim MacDonald and his sister Carmel
landed on the path beside us.

"You better shift yourself," Carmel Mac said, "for
I've just seen Hyland galloping into Baggot Street, said she
was going to get the beggars to do youse up."

"—or Johnny Roscoe," Jim MacDonald added quickly.

About to swing into fast and lively movement, I suddenly hung back.

"Windy!" Carmel Mac's sneer flew snotty.

"Of what?" Annie, halting flight and intention, questioned direct.

"Johnny Roscoe," Jim said.

"Roscoe's a massive fighter," Jim persisted. "Mantle
you with them fists a his, so he would. An he's fifteen," he
added, as if this fact alone should outweigh all others.

And he was also as black as an Arab, I thought. And
he was bigger than me, much bigger. Giddy with sudden
anger, I remembered he also had intelligent eyes, a thick-
lipped, sensuous mouth, a firmly handsome face that was

always dirty, and big hands and broad shoulders topping a slender but powerful body.

"—An is better left alone," Jim said, as if catching the drift of my thoughts.

"But it's not Johnny Roscoe we're after," Annie said.

"Maybe not," Carmel Mac sniffed, "but doesn't Johnny run with Paddy Paddy—an isn't Paddy Paddy Hyland's cousin—so isn't it natural if they take up for her?"

"Why?" Annie stared hard at Carmel Mac, who never actually looked into your face when she spoke, but at some point just above your head.

"Why does *he* always take up for you?" Carmel Mac asked, meaning me.

"That's different," Annie replied, and beside me Jim MacDonald shifted his weight from foot to foot in the little dance that made those watching think he wanted to piss.

"What's different about it?" Carmel Mac eyed Annie's bare feet and scarred knees trimmed by the ragged hem of her red pinny.

"It just is," Annie answered.

"That's the trouble with you," Carmel Mac began, as if gregging a fight. "You think you an him is different from everybody else."

"We are." Annie swiped at her hair, while Carmel Mac touched hers, neatly confined in two poor plaits.

"Me Ma says youse act as if youse were laws unto yourselves," she said, and now I was sure she wanted a fight, and so was Annie.

"When your oulwan isn't carrying her morning mouth in search a beer, she has an awful lot to say for herself," Annie said, and her own voice was clear and quiet.

There was a silent few moments before Carmel Mac withdrew, with an uneasy smile on her sullen face, the resentment that had wizened her eyes. Pulling out, she said,

"Anyway, youse can't win with Paddy Paddy or Johnny Roscoe."

"Maybe not," Annie replied. "But we can have a bloody good try. One thing sure, Maggie Hyland has to be stopped."

"Call the police," a fella passing said.

"Call your mother," Jim Mac shouted after him, and on the steps above us a culchi servant tittered.

"But what'll you do if Roscoe takes up for Hyland?" Jim Mac asked.

"Hang banners on him." Annie pushed her way past two oulwans mouthing, and to a louser loitering she said, "An you shift yourself, buster." She looked back for me.

"Don't go." Jim MacDonald's face was haggard with anxiety. "Roscoe'll kill you."

I glanced from his timid, lonely shaking to Annie, who waited, sturdy and upright, even under the weight of her sack. And then, with a sickened heart, I went toward her.

I had to, I told myself. For I was, with the changes of the morning that Annie had brought about, now totally dependent on the cinders and what I could make on them. And so was she. Between us, we had to have five bob on Saturday. And not just this Saturday, but every Saturday.

But, oh Christ—Johnny Roscoe!

"Come on," Annie said, herself suddenly humorous and going with every step as though toward some savage hilarity, past Jesus, standing with his head bowed beside some joker on the make, and past others who knew what was up and were followed by a few on the go for the diversion a rucky-up promised, and past servants, country girls, all of them, who laughed and gaped, stunned, while those who knew us shouted our names and urged us on. With one eye on them, I kept the other on Annie. Something would happen to divert her, I thought. Something must happen.

My mind overflowed with prayer. Something had to happen. The Poet would come from his plush and plum to bar our way; or Josie, in from the hedge-lined roads under skies that she said were filled with angels, her ears cocked to hear what no one else could; or Lady Callan, who gave us tea and plum cake in a room of books and a marble fireplace; or the three sisters, ghosts, all of them, with their mother, who talked to Annie as if they were still alive, about the clever Helen, the musical Mary, and the beautiful Adelaide; or maybe . . .

Annie's feet were hardly touching the ground, and on the square that morning there wasn't a shagging thing astray. Nothing, in all that commotion, to distract her. And then a woman bawled, and my foot hit something hard and my pace slackened and Annie was in front of me and, behind, I felt a pressure. My feet left the ground and then found it again, and someone told me to hang on to my hat. And then, with a quick wheel, Annie slowed and disorder cleared and we were again running breast to breast, Annie into the fight ahead, where in her mind's eye a cloud of dust was even now showing the anger of it.

"Watch where you're going," she said, and I was, and I told her, but all I could see were the shifting railings, then the dim blue of the sky, but it was no longer over me. And, away in front, the houses soared drunk.

"Shift your sack on to your other shoulder," Annie said, and I did, without stopping, and then the dark of the houses departed, and what I saw then was the dark of eyes under brows that were heavy and coarse. I saw shoulders broad, with long arms stretching into big hands pressed against thighs that I knew were hard and breaking the seams of Johnny Roscoe's longers.

"Anyone but him," I said, and Annie, who could herd mice at a crossroad, said,

"Why, for God's sake?"

"Because . . . ," I said.

"If you're afraid, we can forget it," Annie said.

"I'm not," I said.

"In that case, if I was you, I'd remove that rowdy cowl, for it's hindering our progress."

"I'm not going any quicker," I told her. "An I'm not taking off my hat."

"Don't, then," she said, and, without turning to see, I knew she was eyeing me sharp. "You used to be afraid of Johnny Roscoe," she said.

"Well, I'm not anymore," I replied, and I was glad I hadn't given way on the hat.

"How come you don't want to fight him, then?" she asked, and her voice was cool in a high, offhand way.

"I never said I wouldn't fight him, did I?"

"No, but you're not anxious to," she said. "Well, you don't have to fight him." And, after a while: "I will.

"Although I'd rather not have to," she said quickly, "because he never makes any trouble for me, and he did take us to the pictures, remember?"

I remembered all right, and the way Annie kept changing seats and shouting, "Lights!" It was the first and only time either of us had ever been inside a picture house. And then we were thrown out, but not before Annie had demanded, and got, Johnny Roscoe's money back.

"Now tell us," she said suddenly, "what you're afraid of."

"I'm not afraid," I replied testy. But Annie persisted. "Why don't you want to fight him then? Is it because he took us to the pictures that time?"

"Because—" I said. And I thought, Because I like him and because, round the lane and in the street, nobody ever said they liked anyone or anybody. Annie, who knew me in all things, might've understood. But then there were some things I didn't even share with Annie, and the way I felt about Johnny Roscoe was one of them.

Before, I had been afraid of Johnny Roscoe, but I wasn't now, and hadn't been since that evening in Henry Street. That was the evening when Annie, testing her need of me, or maybe it was mine of her, left me alone to find my own way. It was an evening of carol singers and lights. Of buildings braided with light. Of colors slashing with streaks of red that dimmed to purple even while you were looking, above roof tops and down wide vistas. And it was an evening of delph. Dangerous delph. Cups with the handles missing and saucers and plates cracked and chipped.

In Henry Street certain shops, instead of letting them go for nothing, sold cheap, and we bought, to sell again for a small profit round the street off Rock. That evening we were on business bent and high-spirited as we tore among the people all clawing for foot-room on the crowded pavements. And we were mindless. As fools at first, the pair of us. Blind and bothered to the growls of reprimand that came when we impeded the overbearing and laughed at the pompous. Till it happened. And in fact there was nothing very remarkable about what happened and went on happening. Only the way it happened. Because to begin with it was only contentment of which I was aware. An ease for which I couldn't account and for which I should never have tried. But, passing a drunk on a corner spewing, I tried. Ferreting back on myself to find the cause, the hidden snag, that would show and mock to death this thing inside me. Because the strange peace I was feeling *was* rare and the gaumlike happiness springing out of it, even more so. And neither were to be trusted. Not like that. Not just like that. And then I did know, and with no warning I realized I was loving Annie.

And not in a hurried panting way. And not in a way
that would've made me want to drag her into the first sidestreet we came to. Even if I was thick enough to try. Besides
you can love somebody without it being like that. But in a
way that has wonder in it. Slow wondering. Like you wonder
at a story you've never heard before—or at a sight you've
never seen. There was loneliness in it and a kind of dread
that spoiled a bit because I knew it was something I would
have to keep to myself. This thing that I had never felt for
anything or anybody before. And watching her and hearing
her laugh I knew it meant something to be able to make her
laugh and that it meant even more to be able to make her
face bright when she looked at me.

And thinking this I felt something else. There in the
darkening seconds in Henry Street, it was as if I myself
were one person and the me Annie knew another, and these
two had been streeling down different paths till here in this
street, and this wind, and among those Christmas crowds
the two had come together and merged. For a second I
thought of telling her. Asking her if the difference I was
feeling showed. Have her pause and contemplate with me
this thing that with nobody's help had happened. And I
might have risked it if at that very moment the gray-eyed
girl and the woman with her had not pushed themselves
between us.

I saw the parcels fall and heard the woman's outraged
exclamation. I heard Annie say, "Watch it, Missis," and
knew that, as always, she was getting in her bit before the
other could. I heard the woman say: "We were watching,"
and I saw that *she* was watching both of us, but that the girl
alone was watching me.

"You'll know him the next time," Annie said. "You're
looking at him as if he owed you something," she added,
and the girl was, and to avoid her look and Annie's stare

and to hide my own confusion, I bent and picked up the parcels and handed them over to the girl. She took them and smiled, between the fur of her hat and the fur trimming the collar of her coat.

"Come on," Annie said, and tugged at the sleeve of my gansey. But I couldn't go. Caught by something peculiarly calm and deliberate in the girl's manner, I couldn't take my eyes off her. I felt myself blush, and Annie, who never missed anything, saw; and seeing, Annie, in sudden stubbornness, ran. Later she tried to say she went because she couldn't stand to see the spectacle I was making of myself. But that evening she said nothing, just ran—and I waited, unable to run with her, unable to do anything other than wait for the girl and the woman to go, and when they did go, unable to do other than stand and think about her while I waited for Annie to come back.

A strange girl, and a sad girl. Gray-eyed and gently pretty. A *proper* girl, Annie's mother would've said. A peaceful girl. Made you think of dolls and prams and colored picture books. And without that sense of excitement and commotion that surrounded Annie. The kind of girl who would never have to depend on your unquestioned acceptance of her in all her moods the way Annie did. But then she wouldn't have moods, and if she did, they wouldn't be the shattering stormy moods of Annie. Thinking about her, I was looking up and down the street for someone skinny, fast-walking, and narrow-hipped; but of Annie there wasn't a trace.

I stood. For a long time I stood determined to do nothing, then went to the edge of the path to sit and wait. For her to come back. Annie always came back and always she acted as if she'd never been away. Not that she had to come back but . . . She didn't own me and I didn't own her. We just sort of took up on the canal one day but we don't belong to each other: she's an independent, never wanted to own anything in her life except Ellen Simms' cart. But whether she liked it or not, without me she was a bit like Mary Doyle's crook-neck pullet. The one that ate sideways and was finally pecked to death by all the others because they didn't like the look of it and because it was different.

Annie's different, and that's why nobody but me would put up with her. But then everyone else tries to rope her in. And she won't be roped in. She's like someone who'll give you the most intimate information free, but anything that suggests a direct question, a pinning down, puts her right on her guard. I know this, but others don't, not always, and not at first. And I learnt the hard way. I had to, because right from the first, I needed Annie and she knew it. Needed her very presence in an urgent almost desperate way that was balm to something in her that, till she met me, had been exposed and raw and wanted to be calmed down. I knew this. I also knew that things happen and that human needs change and that few, even our bad ones, are lasting. And supposing Annie changed. Just suppose this once. . . . A disquieting loneliness crept into me as I sat there on the edge of the pavement; and wondering at the nature of this sudden and new kind of doubt I was suffering, I felt the pennies go dead that till now had been making a shrewd jingle in my trouser pocket.

I kept looking up and down the street, afraid to move away from where it was she had left me in case she came back, and all the time expecting to see her stray out of the agitated life cramming the street but nothing happened. Nobody even walked the way she would and nobody with her laugh elbowed aside the crowds crossing north, south east and west whenever traffic gave them the chance of moving. I stayed watching and at the same time felt every muscle in my body tighten in the effort I was making not to tear up and down that street. What I didn't know then was that in other years I would make no such effort.

In other years I would remember this evening as I drifted from corner to corner, uneasy, anxious, looking at every face, into every shop and up to every blinded or lamplit window, looking not for Annie any more but for bits of Annie—on the prowl for some gesture, some sound in others that might have been in the movements of Annie. Or that I would, avoiding the streets I had known with her, stray with frantic loneliness onto the grander ones, packed with traffic and jeweled assertiveness, wanting to but not succeeding in looking confidently aggressive as I touched with my forehead the huge plates of shining glass protecting the food, clothes, and gold-labeled bottles she was no longer around to plunder.

Dublin then would be . . . It would be what it had been before Annie, only worse because now I was older. Before it had been chapel twice a week and floods of people pouring into them. It was gates black and huge and Confraternity men lurking in porches holding out long-handled boxes with slits in them. It was leaflets pinned to Gothically-topped boards telling that Missions were being given and money wanted. It was free propagandists for the Bible operating like Luthers in long dark wet shadows and priests asking when was your last Confession. And Sunday tea, with my mother telling me to hold off and my Aunt Mary telling my Uncle Mick to eat up even while he was cleaning every plate in sight—and when the pennies were plentiful, football with my father in a loving mood up in the freezing wastes of Croke Park—and from my sisters and brothers the thumps brought on by my silences which they didn't like or understand and were afraid of, convinced as they were that sooner or later these same long silences would take me to where none of them would want to follow. But worst of

all, Dublin without Annie would be that awareness of being
a totally alone person and the ponderous weight of the mask
you were forced into wearing to hide it. Only with Annie was
I released from the necessity of posturing, pretending that
I was queer in the Goddamn head for football and working
my balls off for a lousy two shillings a week—and that the
young scrubbers round the street didn't shrivel my guts every
time one of them made a hungry wet-lipped pass at me.
Only with Annie . . .

"Ey! Tucker!" Dazed with looking and moithered
with thought, I didn't see Johnny Roscoe coming till he was
down on his haunches beside me. And then he was telling
me that I looked as if I was being neglected by my dearest
and closest friend. And then I was on my feet moving away
from him and frowning my way back from time with all the
caution of a kid carrying a salt shaker and stalking a bird.
And then I was springing back from him and asking. Asking
him to leave me alone for fuck's sake; and when he wouldn't
I was running from him to a lane into which I ducked to
escape his randy roughing-up.

But he chased me, and catching me, Johnny Roscoe
kissed me. And that's when it happened and that's how it
happened. Just like that up against a wall. No palaver, no
nothing. And I told him to "give over." Once. Because I
thought he was more serious than he should've been and
because I was scared stiff—not of him, but of myself and
the shock running through my body. And to escape the grip
his arms made, and to stop myself from reaching out for
something that, till now, I'd been denied, I started to lash
out at the familiar face gone strange with emotion—and
then, with a blast of anger, he began to smother my mouth
and the sounds of protest I was making with lips that were
hard as hell at first—before they went summer soft.

"You don't have to be frightened," he said once, rough. "You needn't be," he said, and leaned against me, and I waited for my heart to slow down. And then it did, and so did his. And then Roscoe was taken, had taken me in his arms, was overwhelming me with some gigantic need. And I knew I should get the hell out of there but I didn't—instead what I was doing was investing him with Annie's face and even with Annie's body and what I felt back there on the street for Annie I was feeling for him—and all I did then was breathe into the mouth, shutting my eyes, closing each in turn with slow tender pressure before it came back again to my mouth, and into it Annie poured deep moans through which Johnny Roscoe kept telling me not to be afraid.

And I wasn't, and I was surprised he wasn't aware of that, and then Annie went on the heel of some farfetched resentment and I was aware only of him. I heard a fluttering, almost frantic it was, going on behind the cage of his ribs, and I could feel them sharp; and then the thrust began, the terrible thrust of his thighs and the rigid hip bones as the part between them struggled for an easy place and, finding it, I felt him settle, and the beat against me became constant, the rhythm unbroken, that reminded me then of the lane, of the springs of beds heard through locked doors on landings on Sunday afternoons. And then into my hand Johnny Roscoe shoved his great stubborn prick, and what I felt then was panic, and I was afraid—but only of weight and the scalding fury of desperate need.

"Christ," he said; like a victim, over and over, like the responses to a prayer, he murmured, "Christ," beading each "Christ" with threats full-stopped with sworn denials and quick assurances; and through it all the whispered litany that told me not to be afraid. And I wasn't, and I told him,

but he didn't hear, for he was lavishing tenderness on me
in a way nobody ever had before—whispering it with a
voice that confused because it was sad and gentle and unknown, like his mouth, and all I wanted then was time to
think, examine the ways of love—of this kind of love—and
marvel at the giveaway his mouth was and the lie that lay
unsuspected behind its toughness. Afterward, dragged back
to what we knew for certain—and, knowing, I was not
afraid and would never be afraid of him again—I saw that
the Arab-dark grin was shy and that it threw out questions
I wanted to answer, but didn't know how to; and, because I
didn't, I ran from him and the lane, back into Henry Street,
to the dealers, legions of them, shawled and earringed,
white-bibbed and bareheaded, standing behind barrels of
grapes and pyramids of cauliflowers, tomatoes, and cab-
bages, and still looking for Annie and feeling a sorrow that
was tinged with shame and a great bitterness directed at
Annie—stood by one of the dealers standing in the gutter
flaunting streams of tinsel and crimson streamers and singing "Jingle Bells."

"Well?" Annie said, and for the first time ever I felt
herself and her voice intrude like a grievance. "You were
about to tell us," she said, "why it is you're not afraid of
Johnny Roscoe any more?"

"I don't know why I'm not," I told her. But I did. And
so did he as we left Henry Street that evening, and giving
up my search for Annie headed for the painted houses, junk
shops, and factories of the Southern Quays. Almost silent
we went, with him lulled and softened by demands he had
not resisted, and both of us knowing, in the accidental touch
of hands, the answers to the questions that nothing more
than the flick of a glance asked. Once, I saw him put the tip

of his tongue between his lips, as if to stop smiles of pleasure coming to them. And once, on the path, walking by the granite walls of the Liffey, he said:

"About Annie. You won't tell her about us, will you?"

I wouldn't. But I'd a good mind to. Because if she hadn't run off and if that sad girl with the gray eyes hadn't turned up when she did—and if . . .

"No. I won't tell Annie," I said.

"It's all right between us then?" Johnny Roscoe asked. "Sure."

It was all right, but he wanted to hear. He grabbed my shoulder and pulled me back toward him.

"Say it," he said. And his left arm went across my shoulders, and through the worn blue of my gansey I felt his hand angle as if to protect.

"It's all right," I said, and to convince stared up. He looked then the way he did swimming in the canal, and on my shoulder his grip tightened. But at Caple Street bridge, his face changed. It was hard again and set for strife. Out of focus then was the last of the low-hanging, smoldering sun that colored to bronze the polar-white slash of the grin he flung down at me as, with his arm still across my shoulders, we negotiated with lorries, floats, vans, and drays, and made for home.

"Look out," Annie cried, and I was bounced from Johnny Roscoe, from the ruffled waters of the Liffey, the pressure of a hand, and the frenzied squeal of gulls, by the powerful grip of Paddy Paddy.

ℰ5

I saw them coming—the murderous fists at the ends of wrists exposed by retreating sleeves. I saw a red welt like another mouth on a white throat. I saw liquid, animal brown eyes in a scattered face and, shrinking from them, saw a jumping figure just as Paddy Paddy's fists crashed on my mouth. I heard a shuddering intake of breath, then, darkly seen, I saw Annie jump forward in a savage rush. I saw Paddy Paddy strike out with his hands to stem the rush, but they were swept aside and in a flash the taut skin stretched over the bones of his face was drenched with crimson.

I saw surprise and rage shoot into his eyes and then, as he reeled round, I sprang forward and with all the venom and power in my body sent my clenched fist into the spreading wet blob. Making a deep, rasping sound in his throat, he stumbled from me to Annie, who dodged the blow he aimed at her. I saw her hesitate and then, as if against her will, saw her spring forward and send him with the flat of her hands staggering to where Maggie Hyland and the beggars were.

I saw Annie run and reach like lightning to grab Hyland. But Hyland, anticipating the move, shrank further into the gang of beggars who, with Paddy Paddy, had come to back her. From tenements emptied for demolition, where they kipped when the weather was fine, the Plumber and his thin-lipped, bitter-eyed wife had come; and from the street corners and doorways and the cankered pastime of begging pennies, Hunger's Mother, with runts of stoop-shouldered men and other pendulous-breasted women. Made brave with promises of sixpences and shillings to buy the biddy, the meths, and the embalming fluid that stirred their bowels, they had first charged us with darting eyes and grins of cunning; but, braked and trimmed to thought by our defense and Paddy Paddy's collapse, they stood now, stunted and clamp-lipped, venomous and motionless, like a corroding frieze on the facade of a building, while behind them, on the ground, Paddy Paddy tried to staunch with a rag the blood pouring down his face.

Relief—that it was Paddy Paddy and the beggars we had to fight, and not Johnny Roscoe—mingled with the pain from my mouth; and, confused by both emotions, I made a clumsy swipe at the acne-smothered face of the Plumber, who, flinging his arm across my head, back-heeled me against the railings, where I fell heavy and stayed breathless till Annie, with one eye on them and the other on me, brought me to my feet again.

Shattering with sneering shafts the uneasy silence, Annie began on Maggie Hyland, telling her the smart thing to do was to haul feet outa there, and, switching from her to Hunger's Mother, with the little suitcase in her hand, went from her to the Plumber and his wife, who of all the beggars haunting the squares and the roads and streets off them were the most despised, for they were also petty thieves, who colored their lives by conning the aged, the crippled, and the infirm out of wealth only big enough for jam jars. A dear and pretty pair, the Plumber and his wife, Annie said. Sharks, who could con the cross of an ass's back and shake down untold misery wherever they walked. For who, but the Plumber and his barren, Cockney wife, would've harmed poor Kitty Byrne and, while her feet were still lingering stubborn on the cast of her husband's grave, rob her of her life's savings? And who, but the so-called Plumber and his wife, would've left Tom Carney without a roof over his head by tricking him out of the money he had given them to repair it? And I remembered that that was what the Plumber was supposed to be: a builder. And as Annie listed aloud his and his wife's mean, lousy crimes, I remembered old Mrs. Byrne and Tom Carney—and Mad Ella, who the Plumber and his wife had robbed and then chained to a wall like an animal in a room of her own cottage up in Ranalagh. I remembered also what she looked like, the day the neighbors discovered, and the police released, her.

Suddenly misery-filled, I wanted Annie to stop, and the blood to stop running down Paddy Paddy's face. I wanted the beggars to move, for Annie to shift them into movement; to get away from the square, to the canal and Mary Doyle's house, to the pictures of contentment that at that very moment were flickering in front of my mind's eye: pictures of Mary Doyle and her mother, who liked to read the paper for the deaths and the ads, and who liked books, and owned two, and kept hens and stored pears on high shelves. But mostly what I wanted at that very moment was for something long lost to view in Paddy Paddy to loom up— for him to get to his feet, to burst out again and sever, even in fight, the things *he* was raising to irritating life. Anything that would halt the stream of crippling thoughts making their own way back to that black place, and that black morning . . .

Because that was the morning that marked Paddy Paddy's alliance with the beggars. Before that, Paddy Paddy and his brother Alfie had run with us. Until Alfie was killed. After that, Paddy Paddy went a sour way. Always older than us, he stopped running with us and doing the bens. The eldest in a family of nine, he left home and the lane and took to the streets and began to be seen everywhere: loafing about the roads during the day and at night scouring lanes and looking in windows. We heard stories. Paddy Paddy had slashed his throat with a razor blade. Paddy Paddy was hunting drunks and rolling them. Paddy Paddy was killing cats and dogs and stringing them up on clothes lines. And he was seen with the street's pumps, and was taking girls, who were drawn to him: clean-haired and soft-eyed culchies who, new to the city and in a hunger for affection, went with him, and afterwards were left shamed and degraded.

We heard, Annie and I, but we saw him seldom, and when we did, it was always in the distance, knocking senseless those who put difficulties in his way, or with the beggars, or on his own, floating on biddy, embalming fluid, or meths, shouting threats and lost, bewildered things that had no sense. Because Alfie was dead. He died that morning, a red winter morning, digging for coal in the caves under the walls supporting the railway.

Going where nobody went, we went, that morning, Annie and I, with Paddy Paddy and Alfie, down hacked-out steps to a door, and beyond that down more steps, to burrow through heaped, wet slack for the coal Paddy Paddy said was buried underneath. Beautiful coal, Paddy Paddy said. English coal. Keep a fire going for months. And even better

further in, it was, he said. Only to get at that you would
have to go in under the shelf of roof, where you couldn't
stand because the roof was shored up with planks and iron
pieces. But you could if you went in steady under the planks,
Alfie insisted. On our bellies, Paddy Paddy said, doubtful.
Well, that's how we'll do it, Alfie said. And we did. Digging
deeper and deeper to get at the biggest lumps, and then
crawling out backward with our arms full. And laughing.
At Alfie first, and the world he shaped of buried treasure,
of lost pound-notes and rain showers of chocolates stretching from here to China, of streaky rashers and oven-fresh
turnovers. And then laughing at everything, all of us. And
talking—Paddy Paddy about motorbikes and greyhounds
and horses that won every single race. And then all of us
talking together—and then not talking and not laughing,
because after a while the dust was coating the insides of our
mouths and caking hard in our nostrils, so the only thing
said then was, "Move over," and, "Give us a bit a room."

And then, without warning, you were aware of something else, and fright, like a skull, was beginning to smile its
way through the drawn flesh of your face, and your lips,
like a nigger's, was rushing to meet it. Shutting your eyes,
you could feel the rumble, and you knew that could be your
stomach. But there was no mistaking the beat of your heart.

Shivering, because you think it must be terrible to be
dead, you remember all the dead you know and start to
count, starting with Gervaise Mathews, and get as far as
seven, and to fight that, begin to think of the people beside
you. Annie, stretched long and gangling, shouting in angry
loudness that nobody should go in any further. Annie, with
her face between railings, watching ladies' kids in a garden,
admiring quietly and without jealousy their toys and clothes
and unstained skin, while they looked out at her with eyes
like slits in a wall. And Annie, in the streets, urging me on

and on and on, sharpening in me her own painful longing to know more, feel more, discover more. And then, the way now, while I'm trying to breathe deep and give no hint of gasping or panting, she feels—as she always does—my uncertainty, every jerk of slowness, and I am aware—as I always am—of her greater strength as she helps me forward.

And then I think of Paddy Paddy, who is shy and lanky, with gentle manners and nervous ways. Even in the dark I'd know the large bones and broad, high cheeks of his face, and his habit of narrowing his eyes under the ridge of brows when he's looking far away. And in the brown waters of the canal, where he swims like an otter, I see him.

And then Alfie. Alfie smells salty and sharp and sour beside me, and then goes past me. He is ragged and quick. He has red hair and very blue eyes and a secret: he likes dolls—but one in particular, a rag doll that Paddy Paddy bought him. She has black hair and china eyes that open and close. He calls her Lilly, and he keeps her hidden—not only because it's shameful, and the kids would jeer, but because his mother's always in the rats and, like Annie's mother, she pawns and sells everything she gets her claws on. Lilly is kept hidden from everybody except Paddy Paddy and us. At night, she sleeps between Alfie and Paddy Paddy in the bed: in Alfie's arms. And I see him now, edging close to the wall behind a stake, and from overhead whispering little gusts of wind come down through slits we can't see.

"Alfie!" I can hear Paddy Paddy. "Alfie—are you minding what I said?"

But Alfie's not minding. Nobody's minding. Everybody's very quiet and very workmanlike and everybody's clawing forward and forward with a terrible patience.

"Alfie! Alfie! Leave your legs out or I'll burst you. Alfie, do you hear me?"

Above us, a stake sags and settles.

"Come on," Paddy Paddy says now, and his voice is high and strange.

"Ah, just this bit," Alfie begs with slatted eyes.

We stop again, all of us, and listen. And now the rumbling isn't in my stomach. It's overhead for a minute, and then it falls.

It's rock and stone and slidering slime. And it can't be pushed back.

"But if he stays still . . . ," Annie says.

"Stay still, Alfie—don't stir." Paddy Paddy sounds hoarse. "Oh, Christ! Oh, good Jesus—he's gone. Annie, help me."

"We'll get him, Paddy, we'll get him . . . dig in here . . . No, not that way—use your hands!"

And, after a long time: "I can't feel him . . . I can't feel him . . . Alfie . . . Alfie . . . my brother . . . my brother . . ."

"Get help," Annie says.

"I will: I'll go," and I go, to a man taking the winter air between bridges. "Mister, quick, there's a youngfella trapped be the roof. It fell on him," but the man, not wanting to be brave in a strange world, hurries away and I'm left with a dead, quiet feeling, until the sound I can hear mounts to a howl.

After, and long after, while fear slashes our faces, the questions, the chastisements. But first, the pad, the pen in white hands, and you look, from them up to the condemning stares, and from them to the pad again and the clever, sinuous movement of the finely fixed hand holding the pen, weaving lines over the lovely bare whiteness of the paper. And then again, the stupid interference, the jobs that have to be made and kept, because what the hell did they think we were doing down there? Remembering Mr. Cribbens, I

say, "Growing mushrooms," but only Annie thinks it's funny.
The copper threatens: you give me this straight or I'll lug
you and that youngwan down to the bridewell. In the first
place, youse had no right to be down there, trespassing on
private property—it'll be jail and no recompense for this
day's work, so give it to me straight: what happened? And,
Jasus, he's clumsy. "Stand on your own shagging feet," I
shout, jumping from underneath his.

"Nothing happened," Annie tells him. "It just moved,
that's all."

"What moved?"

"The roof."

"You saw it?"

"Course I saw it—I was there, wasn't I?"

Annie shifts her attention. "Take your hands offa him,
he doesn't want to go."

But Paddy Paddy, with blood and dirty tears dripping
down his face, does go, with the man pumping out prayers,
after Alfie, smothered under the fever red of blankets on the
stretcher.

We watch them go from the dark of the railway yard,
Annie and I. And the song comes into my head, the one the
kids sing: Paddy mind the baby, Paddy mind the brat, Paddy
mind the baby, For your mother's in the rats. And then we
walk, in a new, orderly way, from the railway yard to the
canal. To a tree Annie goes, very neat. Words are hard to
form and speak, for a long time. Then Annie says, "Poor
Alfie. Poor little Alfie, with his chocolate rain and his doll."

"He didn't have it with him," I say.

"No, I know. It's under the board in the floor, under
the bed. He keeps it there in the day. I saw his tongue," she
says then, quickly. "It was stiff and black. Every single thing
is ruined. His poor teeth. And poor tongue." Against the
bark of the tree, her mouth begins to hack sounds.

And the dead see nothing, feel nothing, hear nothing, only black. It must be like the inside of coal, I imagine. A boat goes by on a high, muddied swell. A turf boat, and it's loaded. If Annie and I hurried, we could get it at Leeson Street bridge, going through the locks. Lovely hard, red turf. I'd like to cry, but I don't. I'd like to move, but I don't move. Some things can't be lived with. I think of the pink-eens in the canal and the eels and the bloodsuckers, all stunned—and then about the gang of otters that came into it one winter and the Army was sent for to destroy them. The Poet—the one Annie's mother doesn't like—made a big thing of the otters. The enemy was engaged from the north bank, he said. And a whole lot more. The victory was Ire-land's, he said, and everyone laughed, because they were supposed to; big, funny laughs. Balls. In long grass, in run-ners sodden from the wet slack, I wait for Annie, under a sky that's a wide streak of haggard gray, weighed down with big, useless clouds. The boat moves through a hush quiver-ing with voiceless words, while my fingers, numb with cold, grip the mouth of a sack. Over where I guess the sun to be, I can see a cold, steely light, like the slim blade of a knife blood has rusted.

"Okay, Hyland, if you don't want me to wreck every bone in your body, you and the Plumber better vanish," Annie said, and I was brought like a somnambulist from the canal, and the solemn, hovering, ghost-gray presence there, to the square and Paddy Paddy and the silent men-ace of the beggars facing us.

Pushing aside layers of thought and questions, I saw they hadn't moved, and neither had Annie. She stood grip-ping her sack, her face scornful, her gaze heavy with con-tempt for the Plumber and his wife and for the beggars' dumb show she found degrading, her loathing for their bitter, spiteful animosity as they cadged showing in the sturdy way she began to name them, bubbling her boisterous challenges on rising exuberance as she invited each in turn to put the tin hat on her. But none of them did. And I knew that, without Paddy Paddy's ton-heavy fists to back them up, none of them would. They simply stood and waited. Not a shout from one of them, not a fist—nothing but Annie's mocking jibes and, in between, the trot of a horse somewhere, the rattle of bridle and bit; and, over all, the overpowering smell that comes from the shrinking weight of destitution.

And then one of the beggars did move. A stinging spume of spit hit Annie in the eye, and into the chill their silence had cast, and the cold that had settled, they sprang—all seven of them—with a roar into life.

And not with bare hands, but with sticks and stones wrapped in rags and sacks gripped in long, rough, gaunt hands. Like pubs unveiling themselves by sliding the shutters down, the sticks appeared and the stones, as they lashed and hewed with venomous envy and bitter spite, tearing from me shouts and streaks of pain that stretched insect-ridden as with thinning legs they floored me again and again, each time kicking into me, as Hunger's Mother said, visions my guts had never dreamt of. I saw Hyland and felt her get a punch in and heard the Plumber roar at Paddy Paddy to "put a leg under him!" I saw Annie shoot up from a tight bunch bent over her and later, when she brought me from a deep calm into which I was slipping by a shout and something in it that came from her and the obstinate fight going on in her body. Twisting to see I saw her spring out of Hunger's Mother's reach, and then again caught a glimpse of her, with her arms up, sheltering her head and face— and, pushing from the baleful, half-lidded eyes of the Plumber, I tried to reach her, but from his bitter, panting gasps I couldn't budge. I saw Maggie Hyland and heard her scream, "Get her!" to someone I thought must be wan shaken and doubtful, and again heard her say, "Close in!" just as Paddy Paddy flung himself into the fight again.

Now, through the turbulence of fight and fright, I heard Annie's goading reply and I saw her in her red pinny soar like a colored jay up from a flock of crows, just as Paddy Paddy, stuffed with the dust of death, finally put the boot in.

Unbalanced from the pain of blows, it wasn't until we had left Fitzwilliam Square and had reached Leeson Street and the shops along it that I discovered the loss of my hat and coat. And it was only when Annie, with her eyes gleaming and looking as if she had run through storms, pulled me into one of the shops that I remembered Paddy Paddy's hands sliding off me. And it was while Annie, with her face aimed straight ahead, paused just inside the shop and, out of the corner of her eye, worked the place over, like a burglar casing a jewelry store, that I remembered Paddy Paddy jumping to his feet, and then seeing, on the outskirts of my mind, the cinder-pickers.

As we went past stacked tins of paint and pots, pans, kettles, and delph, to the back of the shop, where foodstuffs were sold, I remembered seeing Biddser Mulvey and—as Annie's hand closed on a tin of sardines and then a square of cheese—Bessie the Pig and Brennan the Builder, and Paddy Paddy shouting, "Run!", the shout dying in his throat as he sank without a murmur under Johnny Roscoe's fists.

6

"What I don't remember is getting out of it," I said, and meant the fight, but Annie knew.

"I dragged you out," she said, and her hand bold as thought closed on a loaf on the counter, then came away empty. "And my hat an coat." And following the direction of her gaze, I saw she was staring into a pair of fiery eyes, regarding her from the inner gloom of a room off the shop. "Were bet off you," she said as we reached the door only inches ahead of the long, reaching arm of the shopkeeper.

"Who by?" I asked, as we headed for the full and plenty of Mick O'Brien's grocery store at the bridge.

"Don't you know?" Annie looked at me.

"How would I when most of the time Paddy Paddy and the Plumber were hammering dark shapes into me?"

"Just the same, you shoulda felt something," she said, and with the purposeful look of a hunter she paused just inside the door.

"Well, I didn't." And the fact that I hadn't was suddenly stirring me into a state of alarm. For supposing money was stashed away in the pockets of that coat? Or a pawn ticket?

"But money wasn't," Annie said. "And *your* mother never sends you to the pawn."

"No, but Nan Oxer does, and I don't always remember to hand up the tickets."

"So what's fretting you?"

"Nothing."

"Something is," Annie said.

And something was. The loss of the hat and coat was fretting me. So was the ache in my balls where Paddy Paddy had put the boot in. So was the nausea and short spells of dizziness. And so was Ellen Simms. She'd think I'd sold or pawned the hat and coat, and I'd have to let her, since I couldn't tell her the truth.

"I don't see why not," Annie said. "Even Ellen Simms couldn't've taken on that pack without coming undone."

"We should've," I said. "We have before, and nobody should be that easy to rob."

"Nevertheless, the fact remains," Annie replied. And I could see that, whereas my mind was still restless from the fight and its results, hers was already zigzagging to the shop and the prospects before us.

"And that's what Ellen Simms will say when she hears," I said. "An what about the cart?" I asked. And surprise and a flicker of fear crossed Annie's face. "Because that's going to demand even rougher handling. And are we up to it? That's what Ellen Simms will ask if she hears about this morning. In fact, I bet she thinks twice before parting with it."

"She'll part with it," Annie said: her words chiseled, as if I was deaf. "And when she does, I'll hold onto it."

"Supposing she doesn't?"

"I'll strangle her."

"But you said this morning—" I began.

"This morning nothing. I've changed my mind, that's all."

"In that case, Ellen Simms could change hers."

"Not if she's a grain of sense," Annie snapped. "Besides," and she brought her left foot up her right leg, "Ellen Simms promised."

And on nothing more than the strength of that promise, we had quit our jobs. And if this morning, which so far had been one great improvement on nothing, was anything to go by, we'd been the right pair of gaums. But then, that was the trouble with Annie, this belief she had in the promises of others. She herself seldom made one, but when she did she never broke it, and could never understand it when others did.

It wasn't, but Miz Robey said it was, the only childish thing about her. But then Robey didn't know everything. She didn't know the way Annie felt about gardens. Or youngfellas. Or love, for which she had no time and which, she said, was a great big fake. And wasn't Robey the one who, when the Poet said Annie was the only real live anarchist he had ever known, told us anarchists were Protestants with heart trouble, and took us up to Mount Argus for the relic? Filled now with the gnaw of anger, for which I could find no reasonable place, I found myself suddenly wishing to Christ Ellen Simms had never given me that lousy hat and coat and that she'd kept her mouth shut, for it was she who put this whole notion of being a dealer into Annie's head in the first place.

"Well, we're going to have to try keeping Ellen Simms in ignorance about this morning," I said, wanting to ease the tension I had created between us, but most of all want-

ing an out from the ungainly doubt I'd blemished Annie's
face with.

"We won't have to." Taking her eyes off me for the
first time, Anne swung round and leveled with her stormy
gaze the shop, the stuff, and the people packing it. "Because
I'm getting that hat and coat back," she said, and without
another word, and abrupt with purpose, she moved in. Past
a brown-coated woman assistant who with a Sunday-
curtained gob stood behind the counter on our right she
went and, with supreme indifference, past the bookkeeper,
Mrs. Dunn—a robin with the eyes of a hawk, who rose and
fell like the wind in trees at the very sight of us. Toward
avenues formed by crates and tray of turnips, spuds, and
sprouts she went, ignoring today all that lined her way
and, pausing, did so only to instruct and then only when we
were out of sight of the counter and maneuvering cunningly
among the gentry stocking up from the big houses round.
To begin with, since we had already lost the morning, there
would be no loitering, she said. "Or mitching," she warned,
knowing I loved to among the rich who, out from houses
full of the glitter of silver and the glare of mahogany,
lingered like invalids over goods God never meant us to
have. Neither would there be any ducking or dodging, she
said, and I knew she was thinking of those other shoplifters
who, without her skill and guts, darted into a store and
cowered furtive among legs and skirts and made from time
to time a quick, silent snatch at something useless and then
had to run for it or, if caught, suffer the degrading indignity
of whingeing for mercy on the basis of poverty. Annie
despised this kind of operation and would have nothing
to do with the men, women, and kids who practiced it.
"They make me sick," she'd say. "All they have to do is
what I do." And, though her way took nerve and time, there

was nothing mean or cringing about it, and in the heel of
the hunt it was infinitely more lucrative. Annie always
walked into a shop as if she belonged; took her bearings
in one swift glance; decided as she did so where it was she
wanted to go and, more important, what it was she wanted
to go to; then, showing just the right degree of interest
disinterest, aimed straight for it. Sometimes, depending on
whether we were known or not and on the vigilance of the
shopkeeper and his assistants, she might lose up to twenty
minutes before making her first grab. But then she never
took for the sake of taking—never took what she didn't
need or couldn't use—never left a shop empty-handed—
and so far, she had never been caught.

And that was because she used her head, people said.
And now, as we went past butcher's benches stacked with
cutlets and chops and beef for boiling and beef for roast-
ing, I heard her tell me to use mine, because we had only
this one single intention and "that is to get in and out of
Mick O'Brien's as fast as we can and with as much stuff
as we can carry. So no straying," she said, "or letting your
mind hinder your hands the way it sometimes does, or you'll
have this lot straddling our backs and making mightly
efforts to save our souls and Mick O'Brien's stricken
goods." And her eyes, shadowed but full of desperate
design, flew from me to the shop and the women moving
through it. Sumptuous women and arrogant women, and
Protestants all. They went, the steady and prim, in clothes
that were not of this or any fashion, on slender ankles and
sternly polished shoes, like thistle-seed plumed in the wake
of harlequins—agile and flawless in silk and linen and
razored tweeds; and behind the elegant self-sufficiency of
the powerful and purse-packed, Mick himself, in starched
choker and somber suit, put every face muscle to work in

a big smile, while behind *him* an assistant lagged and with
fawning civility scribbled orders flung in voices we knew
from experience could soar into screams.

Because of a kind of ease that existed between us,
those women we knew and whose bens we did showed
neither surprise nor curiosity at the sight of us. But others,
looking like figurines who had somehow strayed from the
shelves of a scented cabinet, seeing us, dirty-faced and
hungry-eyed, saw something they didn't understand and
from which they must defend themselves, and even hate.
Like Mrs. Kirwan, who had never known the silent terror
of a hungry belly, hurrying now from Annie's glance like
a witch on ringing frost to protect her garden—fruit trees
and flowers that only statues could resist and, until that
night in the Hogans' garden, Annie never could. And Miss
Lemon, who, as a grin broke the seriousness of Annie's
face, turned her back on us to court her smallboned image
in a glass defaced with gilt lettering. With one eye on her,
I saw out of the corner of the other Annie dropping half
a ham into her sack, and as I shoved a four-pound bag of
sugar into mine saw beyond her, in a gaily talking group,
Lady Butler-Burke, who, when the mood was on her, gave
out sweets and geranium shoots, with her antivivisectionist
pamphlets. Annie liked Lady Butler-Burke, who had a
special kind of beauty even if old age was just under the
surface of her skin. But she disliked intensely the Misses
O'Reardons—indefatigable old belles of a hundred balls,
who were greeting us now with stupid expressions of childish waggishness.

Pushing from them and their withering pink-lipped,
dreamy, unrealistic ignorance (they imagined our battle
for survival "capers"), we saw Miss Fay, whose breath
smelled always of gin, standing in her shapeless dress of
striped voile, giving Mrs. Grace Allen, from whom all

weight, fullness, and importance had gone after the death of her husband, an intense account of her sturdy summer, while all the time she smiled cloudy over incidents that had probably not occurred. And then, without warning, we saw across piled tins of Barker's biscuits Mrs. Hogan's hands, hard with rings, reach of a jar of American pickle. Like a street from which the sun has crept quick, darkness came, soured with the scabby dregs of lingering anger.

"It's her," Annie said, and her breath crossing mine blurred the face under the wide-brimmed mourning felt of the woman who, staring at us diamond-eyed, stood like a soldier at attention. American, they said Mrs. Hogan was, but we had never known for sure. Tall and thin and in her sixties—or not yet: there was nothing about her that said. She wrote books for children, or published them. She was an educated, a clever woman, they said. And must have been pretty when she was young. Big and pretty. Her feet were big. Her hands were big, and bright with rings. Seeing her now, I no longer thought about the Pilgrims or Ellen Simms who knew a lot about history, Irish and American, and who had told us about the covered wagons, the ride of Paul Revere, and why the flag had its stars and stripes.

Instead, I thought about the thin seam her lips made in her sallow skin. About Mr. Hogan, who, when he was alive, looked at you out of the gray thicket of his neat beard as if he were all the time weighing up your physical possibilities—even mine. About the words and drawings scrawled in chalk on the path fronting the pink facade and laurel blaze of his great house. About his white head and rich, shining, well-covered body. And about apples that thumped the ground in long grass. And then, as Annie caught Mrs. Hogan's hard glare and held it for a full twenty seconds before letting it go, about the night we finally dared the Hogans' garden, and the thing that happened there.

It was a night in fall, smoky and spiked with the year's first frost, getting in quick, short stabs at my face. A night when hunger cramps, filling us with a fuel of their own on which we could operate, took us from our lane and Rock Street to the heightened silence and sad Protestant remoteness of the tree-lined roads edging the city. A night for hunting and robbing and boxing-the-fox. And at that hour when trees, ragged in a drunken display of the season's fading, purpled and men and the shadows of men, in frayed peaked caps and upturned-collared overcoats, prowled the emptiness on foot and on bikes and muttered dark obscenities as we passed or tried with feverish eyes to lure us into lanes with offers of rides on crossbars and promised pennies.

On Northbrook Road, leaves falling from trees lay idle and curled, desolate on shorn lawns. And in big houses big fires roared in big fireplaces fenced in by big brass fenders, and in polished silences in big rooms frilled-capped servants lit lamps—drew curtains of plush and locked tight brass-armored doors. Behind the houses on one side of the road, the lane into which we had drifted stretched from Ranalagh at one end to Leeson Park and the church the Protestants had lifted at the other. In the lane, girls in caches of clothes gone gray from too much washing stood tethered to fellas who smothered with their mouths the girls' whimpers of ruin. And within bottle-throwing distance of twopenny uprights, loud-voiced in lusty loneliness, tramps like Johnny Forty Coats and Gentle Josie took out years like things from trunks and picked them over for memories as they dragged on butts and counted pennies before settling down for the night.

From the high, barbed-wired walls of the gardens

backing on to the lane, color fled the way it did from the faces that were here and there raised to us as we passed, but in the flowing, red scarf on the woman who had come into the lane before us, color smoldered like blood, or fire.

"And *that's* not just anyone," Annie said as we watched the woman stalking off into the distance. "*That* wan's a lady. Outa one of these houses, And like us, pushing herself forward on the scent of something."

"But what? And at this hour?"

"Right now, we don't care," Annie said. "Thing is to get rid of her, because them wans are great at picking up them telephones and ringing the police. We'll wait," Annie said. And, slowing down to a rambling caution, we did wait, until the woman disappeared. Then, going in the same direction, we headed for the wall and the dense leafage of the Hogans' garden.

As always, Annie, with her superior agility, was over the wall before I was, and by the time I touched ground and was running through shrubs cold with dew toward a maze of saplings, she had already reached the orchard and the trees ripe with the fruit we were after. Laughing back at me, just as I reached her she told me to look, and beyond her, through trees linked with ribbons of silver made by slugs, I saw a lawn smothered under the weight of leaves and above them more leaves fluttering down to half-remembered things of earth. I saw a path unworn and cutting at crazy angles up to a terrace of gray stone, and then a house of long, narrow windows, over which the curtains had not been drawn and through which no light showed. Nevertheless, there would be people somewhere, I thought, looking into the shadows that lay with a greater hush across the house: and because silence had been intensified, thoughts fell loud and came out into the open.

"Maybe," Annie said, but it was the garden, with its

aching wilderness of tangled leaf and fruit that was claim-
ing and holding her attention—and mine, but for different
reasons.

Looking for what I couldn't see, I thought it was
gloomy and, in spite of Annie's shining excitement, full of
sighs and uneasy rustlings, as if men or ghosts watched
us from its outer darkness. And I wanted to go from it
and the sudden sense of unease and the hush that was like
the one that comes before an unknown trouble. But most
of all I wanted to run from the silence caused not by lack
of sounds but by a waiting. And I said so. But Annie, now
that her eyes were no longer shaded by hunger or anxieties,
only laughed, the way I knew she would, and, pointing to
the house, told me to feast my lovely wans on that.

But even the house, for all its upright elegance, seemed
to me to have something wrong with it, and my frown of
uneasiness said so plain. "So it's harboring a ghost in every
room," Annie said, and the smile she flung was tinged with
green and meant to draw. But into her mood I wouldn't
be drawn. All I could do was stand there, stiffened and
waiting, scanning the garden as if seeking something invis-
ible and dangerous; not speaking, not even answering when
what she said demanded an answer; and not moving, either,
even when, with a wild, rising lightness, she began to spread
the sacks at our feet.

Watching her go from tree to tree on footsteps that
after a time slowed to a wander, I began to think it strange
that, whereas even when there was nothing to fear, I was
always an alien in the gardens we invaded, and walked soft
and unsure on the ground under me, something new and
entirely different happened to her. A change came in her
I could never explain. It was as if, during the jump from
the wall to the ground, something happened that took her
from me, and not only from me but from troubles for which

she had no remedy, to where nothing and nobody could follow. It was as if a garden was the goal of some journey, and in one her face lost its set-for-strife look and laughter instead of rebellion bubbled up inside her. Also, something new came into her eyes, and from her voice all protest went. Anger also went: angers large and small, old and recent, left her.

Even the one against her mother, whose spoiling bitterness, dislike, and cold indifference she didn't understand any more than she knew what that dislike was based on. All she knew was there was something in and about her that her mother didn't want to have anything to do with. This awareness of what her mother felt was always just below the surface and was one of the things she had never known how to consider in her mind, any more than she knew how to deal with the threat of the factory or the feeling her family gave her of being a person with no real place in the world or why she felt like a stray, even in the crowded bed she shared with her sisters under the roof her efforts kept over their heads.

Looking at her now, and catching the apple she threw me, after first wiping it on her chest, some of the things Annie felt swirled in my mind and crossed each other the way her angers did, and listing those, they included persons and groups she held a burning anger against: some servants and almost every single policeman she came across. Sometimes the list flourished, till it included telephones, which she said were a sleeveen invention; rent collectors, and Jewmen who pushed blankets, sheets, and holy pictures onto people who couldn't afford them; landlords, and people who were neither rich nor poor—shopkeepers who acted as if she had come to rob them even when she hadn't; all buildings, like chapels and churches, banks and hospitals, whose workings she didn't understand and whose usefulness

she doubted; and at the end of the list, the youngfellas she
fought off and who would never forgive her for the difficulties she put in their way of loving her. But then,
Annie didn't believe in love, never played at it the way
Carmel Mac and youngwans like Maggie Hyland did. She
wouldn't've written notes to youngfellas even if she could
write, and once, when Jim Mac sent her one, she put the
tin hat on him.

Following the turn my thoughts had taken, I didn't hear
at first the question she flung, and when she repeated it I
asked, "Enough what?"

"Why, fruit, of course," she said and dropped on the
ground beside me the load of apples she had gathered in
her pinny.

"What about it?" I asked.

"I was saying," she replied, "there must be enough in
this garden to keep us fed and in business for a month. I
also asked how many fruit trees in this whole orchard?"

"Twenty applers at least," I said. "And pears," I
added.

"But pears bruise easy," she said.

"And some were cherries," I told her. "Only the
cherries are over."

"Even so," she said, "there must be thousands of
apples and them alone should take us through the winter,
and what's left of the flowers see us through Christmas.
But c'mon," she said, "we've wasted enough time." And
as she readied me and herself for a fuller future, I saw her
face in its new way, topping her pinny, glowing like plum
in the long grass that had not been cut. And, caught suddenly on her mood, I heard her laugh. Then, all at once,
her laugh froze, and in me there was a shock as if a knife
thrown had struck and shivered in my chest. At the same
time—and together—we stopped dead in our tracks, unable

to take in what happened. There was somebody in the garden. A shape, a movement, over by a trellis of crimson-elbowed thorns fronting a clump of trees hiding a path that led to where we had not looked.

Strength rolled back, the way water does from a swimmer, and only Annie's hand, like a green nerve on my wrist, kept me upright.

It's the light, A trick of light, or a leaf falling, I thought. Of the wind, maybe, disturbing the sinister quiet. But the garden and everything in its was completely static, rigid, the equation of a garden.

"It's a copper," Annie hissed.

But the shape had been a double one. A dark, double shape. And the picture denting my mind was of two people coming together, and the image so strong I had to remind myself where we were: in a garden, big and unexplored, surrounded by a high wall spiked with broken bottle stumps and rigged with four lines of barbed wire intended to keep people like us out. Only it didn't. A gate was let into the base of the wall. A gate that opened into the lane. A small wicker gate, locked. Gates always were. To get into the garden, you'd have to come through that gate, from the house, or like us take your chances on that wall. And nobody but us had come over that wall.

Annie let go my wrist and together we bent down and gently picked up our sacks. And then we turned, And saw. With the eyes of the vicious searching a face for wounds, we probed, and stared stunned. Annie's breath against the side of my face brushed cold. For there in the garden, not twenty feet away from us, stood two men, like abstracted forms to which shadows had been attached. Two men. One taller than the other. One older than the other. And the taller of the two, with his arm round the other man's shoulders, said:

"I'm tired of all this. I shall tell her. I shall tell her she must go away now."

The dry thread of the voice was one I'd heard before.

"Two men," Annie whispered, "loving."

And they were. You could see when they stopped moving and stood together, swaying a little until they found their foothold, the balance of one so dependent on the other that there was no way of telling where one man ended and the other began. Two men. And in that garden, on leaves that a sudden, sharp, erratic wind was stirring, the taller of the two, thinking himself unseen, went down on his knees in front of the other and an urgent, hungry labor took place. Two men. And the less tidy, younger, and rowdier stood and waited, his hands cradling the head of the kneeling man and the mouth into which he was thrusting himself. Two men. And the younger stepped back after a time, out of the other's reach, and, making a loose, shallow cup of his hand, closed it on his prick. In the light that endured, he stood and watched steady the older man. Then, arching back, he brought his head forward to see his own body's richness, with its bluish undertones of snow and marble, burst upward on release before it poured sulkily down onto the indifferent earth. Two men. And the one on his knees cried out and up at the propitiating smile of the man on his feet, or his soul did, and another in distress echoed it somewhere in the great house or in the garden in the dark.

I heard Annie's breath begin, and in the seconds that began to flow again something or someone moved in the shrubs screening the gate. A cat, maybe, or in the lane a kid like us was pitching stone. I looked at Annie, but she remained motionless, suspended, unable to move back or forth. And then she did move, silent except for the friction of cotton on brown skin. From me and them she went, as if from some unspeakable mystery.

"Only two men," I said, following her. "That's all," I added, wanting to repair possible damage, while across my mind slanted remembrances of things heard and the scrawl of chalked things seen.

"One of *them* smells of cigars, hair oil, and leather," I whispered and waited to be asked, "Which one?" and when I wasn't I said, "Mr. Hogan does," for that's who the man on his knees was.

Annie's face, though serious, reflected nothing, but her shoulders under her pinny were high and set tense. "I'm off," she said.

"But the apples—" I began.

"We'll do without them," she said, and although sweat showed on her face, she somehow looked cold.

"We'll come back tomorrow night, then," I said.

And we did. But that first night all we did was go from that garden empty-handed, Annie in silence and me burdened with nothing more substantial than thoughts broken and scattered, about Mr. Hogan and the rough he had finally selected from the hordes roaming the roads. And going over the wall and dropping down into the lane, we came face to face with Mrs. Hogan.

Not hiding, the way Mrs. Kirwan and the rest of the gentry did when they tried to trap us as we left a garden. And not pouncing with a moistened hiss, the way Miss Lemon did and as we expected Mrs. Hogan would. But just standing untouchable in a shroud of silence, and looking not at us but at some other situation altogether, and, from the cut of her, one in which there wasn't much hope.

Eyeing her, we backed from her, straightening ourselves as we did so and *waiting*—to be noticed, to shout down the crimes she was bound to allege against us. And at the same time, thanking Christ we carried nothing and that our sacks were empty.

But she didn't accuse. All she did was stand in a tweed-warmed stupor, her arms tight against her sides, her spine backed hard against her own stone wall.

"Sick," Annie ventured, but only after the shock of the meeting had eased up some.

But the devil a sick, I thought into the fear that with Mrs. Hogan's silence was beginning to take possession. Women like Mrs. Hogan don't get sick in lanes. There was no need. Besides, I could see, in spite of my fear, that the disturbance Mrs. Hogan's dark eyes were sucking us into wasn't sickness.

"What, then?" Annie asked, and pity, I knew, was stirring and would any minute now be making her stubborn.

I didn't know, and I said so. Shriveled, even shrunken, in her tweeds and the crimson silk scarf at her throat, Mrs. Hogan was. But not sick; at least, not stomach sick.

"She must be." Annie bent on denying me my senses, and only because Mrs. Hogan was acting as if we weren't within miles of her. So maybe we weren't, but Mrs. Hogan wasn't standing in that lane, either, for even as Annie spoke I remembered the red scarf we had seen on the woman in the lane, and I knew instantly where it was Mrs. Hogan had put herself. Mrs. Hogan was on the garden side of her own stone wall, that's where Mrs. Hogan was: hearing what we had heard and seeing what we had seen, except that, from the look of her, *her* eyes would never be used for ordinary sights again. And it wasn't sickness crippling Mrs. Hogan. It was disgust. Disgust, plain and simple. A deadly disgust, disfiguring Mrs. Hogan's face, until it changed: and her expression then seemed to contract till it reached some point that went way beyond disgust and rage, and even pain. And a loud cry, strong and clear, tore from Mrs. Hogan—and, turning her face to the wall, she let the bricks take it.

We could hear, then, her teeth begin to grate. Like

teeth on teeth, the sound was, till Annie moved. Half a step
she took in front of me, and in quick anxiety she went
toward Mrs. Hogan. I could almost feel her heart against
my own, and I shivered, the way I did when Miz Robey
let me hold the ashes of Mr. Robey in my arms. And then
my hands begged and my voice swam up as my hair bristled,
and in the lane the encroaching dark was flung back and
the light, like teeth, bared itself to consume. I spoke again,
but Annie went on as if I hadn't. I could hear her feet,
narrow and bony, splaying on gravel, and the snarl of twigs
under them snapped. I heard her say, "Mrs.——" and add,
"Ma'am," and I wanted to shout, "Look out!" and I did,
but late, for the sound Annie was making was already off-
guard and as soft as the smile on a sleeper's mouth.

I saw her touch the tweed elbow. And then I saw the
tweed elbow shoot out and strike, like a streel, like an
upright belting a man begging love. Mrs. Hogan struck
Annie's hand from her. I saw the clean creases in the clean
tweed sleeve, and Annie's unbelieving stare and, in the
depths of her eyes, the shocked and stricken look was plain,
and awful. Backing from my sudden venom, Mrs. Hogan's
mouth twisted open, but to the side, as if it were going
to or had already displaced itself permanently. And words
only half understood came through what was only a gap—
words I couldn't make out but, mulling over after, I thought
she must've been saving a long time, for they were all heavy
and coarse and swollen. I saw her stop and rub hard the
arm Annie had touched. And then she turned, Mrs. Hogan
did, as if nothing had happened. And walked away. Through
our stares she went, stretched thin, like the last of bread.
And straight. Like a dead saint.

Annie never asked why. And now, as I watched Mrs.
Hogan pause to speak to the Misses O'Reardons before
moving on to Miss Lemon, and from her to Lady Butler-

Burke, I remembered she hadn't. Not even after the sickness from the force used had passed. And, coming now from the fullness of remembered rage, back to her going through a gauntlet of shelves, her lips thoughtful, her eyes wide for suggestion and opportunity, I decided that maybe it was because motives, even lousy ones, are not always difficult to understand. Except some—for, as I saw her linger longingly over a barrel of pickling pork, which was her favorite food and her death test, I concluded hers were. Because, while I was shocked out of all hesitation and respect by Mrs. Hogan's action and wanted to strike back at her through the only way I knew, Annie herself didn't want to do anything at all about it, and, what's more, said so as we left the lane that night and, back on the Northbrook Road, were turning our feet toward home.

"But I don't want to get my own back on her," she said. "All I want is never to see her or her garden again."

But I did, and by the time we reached Rock Street and our own lane and the dark of our own hall, fury had stirred itself from buried depths and was working its way upward to the slender roots of all my peace.

"Tomorrow night I'm going back to the Hogans' garden, and this time I'll leave it a ruin," I said.

"Well, you'll ruin it alone," Annie replied. "Because I'm not going with you." And in the dark of our hall, we just drew apart as always, without saying good night.

And I did go back to the Hogans' garden, and in spite of not wanting to, Annie came with me. Through the tinselry of frost, the following night, foot-dragging and in one of her, "if you stay quiet, you can hear the angels singing" moods, and me like the brambles at which I hacked, hand-biting, ill-tempered, and mean, already guilty of a murder to which blood would be only an accompaniment, and mauling in my mind's eye shrubs, plants, fruit, and

flowers that in defiance of the frost were still signaling a
final seduction in the Hogans' garden, before I fixed, as I
intended to, my attention on the house and the woman
living in it.

This time, going over the wall, Annie came behind
me and, trailing, said she could smell winter in the distance
as we went toward the orchard and the fruit, which failed
to get her attention and which I noticed for the first time
was in the full flush of its scarlet maturity, except for the
odd pear, and that was only a day or two away from it.
The garden, feeling empty tonight and unaware of our in-
trusion, sent up smells of leaves and rot and fruit and last
flowers, but the courage of its appearing and disappearing
tints seemed tinged with despair.

Thick and black as stout, we heard a man's voice
singing somewhere and stopped to listen, just as from the
house itself sounds which we couldn't at first distinguish
floated.

"Let's start." Annie, not anxious to destroy because
she had made it perfectly clear she would ruin nothing,
spoke just as the sad, dark voice of the man died away and
another, coming from the house, rose in livelier song.

"We'll begin on the apples," I said, loud, in an effort
to prevent the voice and the song and the sad heart of the
garden bringing disorder to my plans.

"On this tree, then," Annie, adrift among the apple
trees, spoke, and her hands, which she never knew what
to do with, waited to touch.

"In a minute," I said, and edging past her went through
the trees to the lawn, to look and place the music and the
voices coming at us through the darkening seconds. It was
a hooley, and I said so back to Annie, who, after a minute,
came slipping through the trees and stood breathing beside me.

"The gentry don't have hooleys," she said. "Only parties and balls and dances," and her voice and her breath reassured like the touch of hands as we stood and gazed like paupered ghosts up at the house from which, tonight, light streamed.

In the oval drawing-room, on garden level, people had been arranged. And under a chandelier that would've frightened age away and lit the whole of our lane and every room in it, immaculate men in sonorous black and women half-hidden in folds of taffeta and clouds of tulle sipped from glasses. In an upright leather chair, a man, like an Inquisitor passing judgment on souls, sat surrounded by women encased in the brilliance of silk at its evening best; and among furniture pushed back along the edges of the room, others in groups stood or sat alone. Through them two servants, streamered and capped, went as if with discoveries of what looked like dishes of sweets and crystallized fruits; and, just outside the glitter of glass and blaze of jewels, a man sat at a piano, and beside him a woman who had reached that stretch of years for which she had chosen flatness stood tossing out music from what Annie insisted on calling a fiddle. Toward them we saw a woman sail, whose face tonight gave no clue whatever to the things we knew to be sewn up inside. She carried a fan and wore a green dress frothing flounces that swept the floor. She whispered something to the flat woman, whose dress of coffee-colored lace contradicted the authority of fashion, and who quickly brought her playing to a stop.

Then everybody clapped, and suddenly, through the thicket of beginning conversations through which you knew colored snippets flew, the flat woman began another tune, and the woman in the green dress began to sing.

"Oh, Come let us go to the ball," Mrs. Hogan sang,

and tapped with her fan. "Music and merriment call," she sang. And she would break off and sing and break off and look at those who had begun to dance. "Gallant young lovers and laughing gels," Mrs. Hogan sang, and round her outspread drifts of tulle flowed like the spray of water.

Wanting to follow on a mad urge where the suave pouring of the water led, I felt Annie beside me tug rough and heard the loss of patience in the intake of breath.

"Watching that lot was not what we came here to do," she said and with the searching hand of life brought me back to the garden and the darkness pressing down. "And something else," she said, taking command. "We want nothing off the ground—fresh off the trees is all."

And in the house Mrs. Hogan began, after loud requests, the song all over again. Turning from it and sweeping the garden in a quick glance, I saw the trellis backed by the trees that hid from sight the path that led to where we had not looked the night before. And seeing it, my thoughts went toward it. It was from there that Mr. Hogan and his rough had come. I went, going over layers of leaves, to the path's isolated darkness that somehow seemed to encourage exposure and then contain it with all the indifference of zinc.

"You're just wasting time," Annie said.

I halted, but the mystery of the path remained. It would take two minutes to see where it went and to what it led.

"A cell in Mountjoy for the pair of us," Annie said.

And inside they were playing "The Blue Danube."

"Just a dekko," I pleaded, and after a slight hesitation Annie gave in and followed me onto the path that went between trees I couldn't name and those I could, like the scrawny pines whose ragged branches mingled overhead.

"It's pitch," Annie said, but light sifting through the trees came from the long, narrow windows of the house and spattered the path and the trees in patches.

"There might be a good kitchen garden at the end of this," I said, to encourage. "Or a summerhouse, like the one in Mrs. Kirwan's garden."

"I doubt it," Annie said. "And anyway—" she began, and broke off abruptly.

We had come to a curve in the path and a tree much older than the others, and bigger, and for some reason set back from them. And, arrested in the middle of a step, we stood looking at it.

Calmly and without panic we looked. The music came back, closed in with the shriked whistle of a bird, then traveled on into other worlds. Here and there a single gold leaf trembled on the black branches of the trees above the face of the man we were looking at.

"It's him, isn't it?" Annie said.

And the light cutting through the trees caught this one and slashed in half the bearded face of the man hanging from it.

"Yes, that's him," I said, and my voice sounded in my own ears like the stale cry coming out of the looking glass in a familiar nightmare.

"The poor long man," Annie said.

In death, Mr. Hogan *was* a long man: a long man in the grip of some terrible emotion, swaying easily where he hung. I didn't want to see his eyes, but I saw them, fixed on us in black penetration. There was knowledge in the face, a long and painful knowing, and in the downward slope of the head a sad pity, sprung from the very foundations of time. Instead of the branches of the trees, the faces of every man, woman, and child who had ever been born might have made a backdrop for him, without seeming the least bit strange.

"What made him do that?" Annie asked, and the music came back again, and a bird somewhere sent and thrilled its grief across it.

"I don't know," I said in the sudden silence.

"Should we tell Mrs. Hogan?" Annie asked, and I remembered how Mrs. Hogan had hacked at her the night before.

I shook my head. "Let her find him," I said.

And we backed and turned to go; and going, the garden seemed to spread as we tore through it.

Later I went back to the Hogans' garden, but Annie never did; which wasn't surprising. What was, though, was the way she stopped doing the gardens altogether. Even Mrs. Kirwan's, whose blossoming loneliness she had always loved. Now she shrank from them, and when we boxed-the-fox, it was me who went over the wall and threw whatever it was we happened to be after over to her. She herself wouldn't set foot in one. And "for no reason," she said when I first asked. Which was a lie, for Annie had always loved the gardens and the greening dark and coppered depths and the secret corners she was always discovering and challenging me to find. And though the streets were her first love, it was to the gardens she ran when the streets began to hurt.

So what, then, stopped her doing the gardens and left in me a sense of something terribly gone wrong? At first, I thought it was the shock of our meeting with Mrs. Hogan, and its outcome, or finding Mr. Hogan dead, or maybe even the strange sin we had seen him commit and which was the one incident she never so much as mentioned. Now, as I fol-

lowed her through Mick O'Brien's, I grabbed all three possibilities, till things seen and known unraveled in my mind
and I knew I was on the wrong track.

In the first place, Mrs. Hogan's reaction that night
had been predictable and, as Annie said afterward, we had
been called guttersnipes by Mrs. Hogan's betters. And as
for finding Mr. Hogan dead, that was nothing to write home
about, either: we had found many a man and woman dead
in the canal, floating face down on a Sunday morning, so
that death was no stranger to us, and neither was it the
savage intruder the Poet said it was. Besides, we'd grown
up with death, had followed many a coffin, aglitter with
brass, through the black iron gates of Mount Jerome, the
lids sprouting blossoms in an effort to smile away the pain
beneath.

And hadn't Annie herself carried from the dead house
of St. Ultan's what was left of the baby that preceded the
birth of the twins? On a December morning, under the
leaden sky that paneled the heavens, while her mother and
father sat dumb, motionless and helpless among the ruins
of the room, it was Annie who went and took the doctor's
failure from the slab in the dead house and lugged it in its
little white plywood coffin, tender and on foot, up the long
length of the two canals to the grave in Mount Jerome.

And as for the sin we had seen Mr. Hogan commit,
I didn't know if it was a sin, and neither did Annie, since,
to my certain knowledge, she had never shared in her life
the general opinion on anything. Any more than the last
person she spoke to was right: they weren't.

Seeing her haul a fair-sized piece of pickling pork out
of the barrel she was idling over, I remembered that, when
she was dead and coffined, I was to wave a plate of pickled
pork under her nose, just to be sure there was no mistake—
for, if there was a breath of life in her, she'd sit up and eat,

she said, but if she didn't, then who liked could nail her down.

I wondered if she was selling the pork as I watched her wrap it up in a piece of paper before dropping it into her sack. And I heard her tell me she had to.

"But why not pamper yourself and keep it?" I asked.

"I can't," she said. "Not if I'm to make the money we need by Saturday. Besides, that's a good six or seven shillings' worth of meat there," she added, and her voice gave way to the slip that I was continuing to make into my search for deeper causes.

Seizing first on one notion, then another, I finally took from the tangle of turning possibilities Mr. Hogan, and this time the thought was not a glancing one—it lingered, the way my mother's belief in the power of prayers did, and stuck, and did not go away. How the next thought occurred, I couldn't say, but looking behind that thin membrane that just about separates experience from intuition, I knew what it was preventing her from doing the garden, and what it was Mr. Hogan had done wrong.

He had brought the lanes and the streets and the people from them into the garden that night; had come with the stained, soured, troubled dark of halls and rooms and beds that sagged and sounds in the night it took a long time to place. Like a pied piper, he had brought the kids, sly and furtive, who grabbed and in a game of house said this was the way; and the youngfellas, sprouting precious first pubic hairs and who, feeling their oats, gazed dark and tormented and dribbled hot juice that looked like barley water from every pore and with convulsive motions exposed themselves to the glare of her vision as they slammed those meeker youngwans against a wall and dug with stumpy fingers and threatened them with soft lips into a kind of submission as they tore with frantic, brutal hurry at their bodies. Into the

dusky grandeur of his own garden, Mr. Hogan had come
with the weight of movement—the slow, drawing sounds of
clothes, the metallic snap of a buckle on a belt; and that
smell, that cloyed sweet, like sick, that lay most mornings
like a caul across Mrs. Murphy's face. Mr. Hogan and his
rough had, with their presence and their strange act, de-
prived her of her only escape, by making the garden real.

"You're wandering," Annie said, and like a man coming from a drunken bout, cross-eyed with tawdry visions,
she brought me from the full stream of minutes passing
back to Mick O'Brien's, to the smell of grapes rank in saw-
dust, and the bitter, hungry-making tang of brine, to a
mountain of butter colding on white marble.

"We need a couple of pounds of that," she said, and
handed me the two-ribbed wooden butter hands that had
been standing in a stone jar of cold water. I dug into the
butter. "Only go easy," she said, and, going easy, I didn't
hear her whispered warning till it was too late. Looking
then where she was, I stared, hoping the woman watching
might be a potential ally.

I saw her wide, straw-brimmed hat, strewn with a confusion of reds and pinks and blue organdy roses, and tried
a smile as blameless as water. But there was no answering
smile. All she did was glare, with that undisguised hostility
peculiar to Dubliners, before she hurried away.

"That wan's out to put the skids under us," Annie said,
and her grin, about to spread into a smile, vanished, and
spinning round I saw, against the door and the blazing
street, Mick O'Brien himself.

"We're caught," I said, as Mick, bleating like a sheep
with the staggers, began his charge toward us.

"We are not," Annie hissed and drew up beside me.
"We still have to get that butter," she said.

"Oh God, not now!"

"Yes, now," she replied.

"How?" I asked.

"I'll catch that man's eyes," she said, And she did. Full on she caught Mick's glare and then, using one of her best and oldest tricks and one that never failed, she directed her gaze past Mick and her eyes widened and her mouth fell open as if she was staring, not at him any more but at some terrible sight beyond and behind him. Mick stopped dead and with his hands still out in front of him, half turned to look back, and so did everyone else in the shop, just as Annie knew he and they would, and at that precise second she made her final grab.

"It's the butter," she said. "I have it," she added. And she did. Four whole pounds of butter. Even as Mick was bellowing toward us and under the eyes of practically everybody else in that shop she had made her last grab without being seen.

"It worked," she said. Thank God, I thought and caught the flash of her grin—then swinging into action, she slung her sack up onto her shoulder. And now with no time for further thought, but looking as blank of design and possession as she could, she started toward him.

Tightening the muscles in my legs, I followed her. I saw Miss Lemon sidestep stiffly, as if afraid of hindering the passage of sleepwalkers around whom the darkness still lapped. And then the bitch who had informed on us, strutting like a culchi jobber, wide-faced and satisfied. I saw the Misses O'Reardons, looking like kids with toy rifles aiming at clay ducks, and beside them other women and assistants gathering to watch and speak, some embarrassed, others surprised. And standing on her own, in her mourning black, Mrs. Hogan's gaze slipped and fell and was still falling when she turned her face away as if to hide a scar. I saw Miss Fay, floating and smiling, the smile of someone on a railway platform to whom you should've spoken while there was still time. And then I shuddered and braced, just as Mick O'Brien loomed into view.

"Thieves!" his ponderous breath screamed, and for a minute he appeared to slant. I could see the flare of his nostrils as his face rose from the frozen white depths of his wing collar, and immediately I thought of horses on a merry-go-round, just as he and Annie faced each other in what was one long and dangerous moment of locked eyes. I saw Annie pull herself upright, and Mick's mouth give a series of quick jerks, and felt above us the old-fashioned electric fan turn slow its warm, stale waves of breeze.

And then Annie said calmly, "Now," and under the cracked effort Mick made to grab we went, and came up like bad pennies on the other side.

From the door, we looked back to see the commotion caused by the shrill screams of Mrs. Dunn, the bookkeeper. I could see her eyelashes, pale as a goat's, and her tongue, clapping between her lips, silent suddenly under the deeper, almost keening, shouts of Mick, who even while we watched began to bawl like a drunk an unsteady way home.

"C'mon." Annie's voice and grin mocked.

"To the canal?" I asked.

"To sell," she said. And with rash and lovely confidence, she hit the street.

7

Thorny-worded the morning was and Friday, and under my hands lathering her back and shoulders Annie stood. Because this was something in which we indulged, we were in the canal standing hip high in the water, taking it in turn to cover each other with muck. Up from us at the bridge kids practiced belly-flops and on the far bank a woman with the face of Lincoln hacked at nettles from which we knew she made cures. Small and sprightly, she had shorn white hair and wore boots and a summery calico dress and every now and then she flung at us snatches of songs that today we didn't join her in. Instead Annie, having begun the morning with a stern, purposeful marshaling of forces to work out the next move and think up new schemes for our survival, was now lamenting the week's losses as I listed them.

"To begin with all that stuff from Mick O'Brien's was a dead loss," she said.

"Only because we practically gave it away," I replied.

"For instance, you let that ham go to Miz Robey last night. An that was worth a quare few bob."

"I know," Annie said. "And so was that pickled pork and we weren't paid for that either."

"And what about Jesus and the slab of rich cake?" I said. "And—"

"But he likes rich cake," she interrupted, and turned to face me so I could rub the muck into her chest and across her breasts.

"Sure he does. And Miss Maher and her father have a graw for pickled pork," I said coldly and stooped to scoop up another handful of muck.

"I know," Annie said, and to excuse her own weakness, "but I couldn't hound Miss Maher."

"We couldn't hound Mary Doyle or her mother, either," I said, "and they got four pounds of sugar and half a dozen candles. And while we're at it, what about the Christkillers—Jerry Barry and his father?"

"So okay," Annie said, "we left old troubles only to grab new ones. But just let's take Mary Doyle first. Soon it's going to be taffy-apple weather and Mary Doyle will be needing that sugar."

"Why, if we're not round to sell them for her?" I asked, and added: "And who's going to supply her with the apples?"

"We will. One of us will," Annie said. "We always have. She depends on us. And as for Jerry Barry and his father . . . well, Jerry hasn't done a hand's turn since they closed down that Jew butchers in Camden Street—and eggs, which *if* you remember is what we gave Jerry, are good for the sick, and Jerry's father's sick."

"So is Bessie the Pig," I said, and she was, and at this very minute above in a bed in the Union.

"Ah, but the nuns who run that kip are a bitter-faced

lot," Annie said. "That pack are not going to destroy themselves or strain the linings of their pockets by giving people like Bessie butter. And God help her, she likes a bit on her bread."

And now it was me being lathered and Annie was doing the bending down and scooping up. "But we still didn't have to give Bessie two whole pounds of butter," I said; and Annie covering me was doing so tender.

"Bessie can swap some of that butter for snuff. And in case you've forgotten, Bessie is one of our best friends and we just couldn't've asked her to pay."

"Or Primmy Maggott's mother?" I said, tilting my chin so's Annie could get under it. "Or Nan Oxer for the two-pound pot of jam?" I said—although I had, unbeknownst to Annie, tried to get Nan to part with something—and last thing last night and again this morning I'd gone knocking on Miss Maher's door; but all she'd done was leave me standing reverent on her doorstep

"What all them people owe still doesn't amount," Annie said.

"Maybe not, but you have to admit it would be a great help right now," I said, and turning my back so's she could get at it, remembered the two shillings my mother would be expecting Saturday night.

"Well, we did ask," Annie said.

"But not often enough," I replied.

"People," Annie said, "can't give what they haven't got."

"Except some weren't even asked," I said.

"Only because I was sure we would make on the ham we gave Miz Robey what we lost on them," Annie said. "Robey could've afforded to pay us for that ham. She's not broke. She's not like us or them other people. She's not living from day to day or from hand to mouth." Annie paused.

"It's funny the way people who have money never believe others can be broke. Not real broke. I mean, look at that money-lender—the foreign woman. . . ."

"The Austrian," I said.

Annie nodded. "Well, I bet her belly has never stuck to her back with hunger. That woman must be seventy if she's a day, and she's rolling—in fact she'll never live to spend what she has—and she can't take it with her, that's for sure; yet she spends most of her life or what's left of it hauling creatures who've only borrowed shillings and pounds into every court in this country . . . How that woman can create the misery she does and still enjoy the comfort of her bed is something I don't understand. As for Robey . . . Well, I did have my doubts about her even as I was handing that ham over to her last night, but I never thought . . . I never really believed she would be mean enough to trick us out of paying for it."

And yet she should've, I thought as I followed her out into the middle of the canal, the pair of us caked with muck and wading deeper into the depths and the swifter current and the pneumonia-making coldness of it—because for years Annie and Miz Robey had been trying to best each other, and between the pair of them there was always ructions. Whorey-looking and dark-skinned, Miz Robey had gold teeth and a voice as thick as blotting paper. She wore rings. A single gold plain or diamond studded ring on every finger of both hands as a guard against rheumatism—and from her ears fringed loops of heavy solid gold hung. A handsome woman striding through middle age, there was still about her something both lovely and obscene, and as Annie frothed the water round us and disturbed armadas of pinkeens, I thought of Miz Robey drunk. Always, just a little, from the very first day she arrived in Rock Street in Alex Cullen's cab, and with what she called her "girls" trailing in shabby hopefulness in another, and describing herself as a widow woman, with the ashes of the late *Mister* Robey in a brass-trimmed casket in her arms.

Back in Dublin from gorgeous experiences gained elsewhere, there was about her an air of revelry and decaying loveliness—and looking at her people said you wouldn't know she was a whorehouse keeper—"Or the meanest oul bitch in the world," Annie would add after we got to know her. And you wouldn't. Instead, seeing her, I used to think about plates of fried bread and the framed oval panels of colored shepherds and shepherdesses surrounded by baa-ing sheep that Nan Oxer had on the wall over her mantelpiece. Some days, looking at her, I even thought about sucking babies—but, if Miz Robey had ever borne any, she'd done so in secret, and they hadn't dragged her down. She took care of herself and was well covered and walked upright, with a lot of confidence in her big body.

But it was the casket that caught and held our attention, and she knew it, and used it. For, because it came between her and her rest to actually part with a penny, she would, instead of paying Annie for scrubbing down the steps or me for cleaning the windows, lead us like pilgrims down into the basement, where we took it in turns to hold the casket in our arms.

"You kids just gotta understand," she'd say, her white forehead cracking in a black frown whenever we asked her to give us a look, "but what's in that casket's all's left of *Mister* Robey, an is, without fear of reprisal, God, or contradiction, my most precious possession. In fact, if the Pope hisself or some mighty-mitered bishop was to lure me to the feet of Christ this minute, and he were to ask: 'Miz Robey, ma'am, what's just about the most valuable thing you got?' I'd point right to that there casket an say: 'That, sweet suffering Jesus—just that. Just that man's ashes.'

"Why, it's like stumbling across a cowboy seven nights a week," she said once after four glasses of the port that warmed the cockles, "having that man's ashes right down here under the callous tramp a them hoors' feet. Only, a course, better than any steamer, because sealed up there is not just money, but islands from which that man still sings love songs to me. Understand?"

And we understood, Annie and me. We also understood she could borrow from certain shopkeepers, and even some dealers, on the strength of those islands, and that possession of them took, to a great extent, the harm out of her and her girls.

"The creature can't be wholly bad," my mother used to say, weighing up the late Mr. Robey against the paint, the powder, the fox furs locked in savage combat on her shoulders, the Parma violets, and the dyed red hair.

"Except about money," Annie would say always, adding: "About money Miz Robey's a Jew."

Now in the canal, and coming up from skimming the pitch weed floor, I heard Annie through a flash, a flutter, an ecstasy of shrillings, telling me to look for God's sake; and dragging myself from memory's frozen gaze, looked into the lemony sun and saw, even as Annie told me to see, on the bank behind us, all of Miz Robey herself. I saw the frayed green taffeta coat first and then her hat and its ragged roses and knew they were shedding petals as she lifted her head to sniff the direction Annie's shouts were coming from—and then I saw her find us and, at Annie's "C'mon," to me, saw her give her slow, big, and all-gold smile.

Sly and slow and non-commital, she watched our shakes and shivers as we climbed up onto the bank and, as if she knew what we had to say, spoke before we could. "It's my last remaining pleasure," she said, "discovering the natural wonders of an unnatural world." She smiled and peered through the straggle of her own mauled beauty for a glimpse of Annie's. "All right," she said, "my last but one." She sighed sudden. "I've just this minute left two wans I used to know up at the bridge. Haven't seen either of them for years. In fact not since I sprained my ankle doing curtseys to Picasso. And that was a long time ago. On their way into Quinlan's pub they were to drink a health to her Majesy and the Commonwealth Games. Wanted me to join them and when I wouldn't were convinced I'd come out to hustle what the tide had washed up. It wouldn't've been a halfport of use my telling them otherwise—or that I was out braving the elements, the genteel and the eminent like yourselves, only because I still suffer the illusion exercise is good for me."

"And isn't it?" Annie asked.

"I haven't yet decided, and I take myself too seriously to hurry matters," Miz Robey said. She looked up at the sky. "I've always thought day light was a great destroyer of a woman's pretensions," she said, "and there's something not right about that sun and the mad glare it's making. It's the God damn dog days. I cut me hand last night opening a bottle for me one and only customer. Thing is it won't heal now till the dog days are over. Because the season of dog days are like that you know. Of course as a rule nothing happens but if it does, or a change occurs, then the change remains till the dog days are over. Things done are not undone, and a mistake made is never rectified."

"Like the monumental mistake we made in letting you have that ham last night," Annie said.

But Miz Robey ignored this. "Littered with mistakes this peculiar summer is," she said, "which if the truth be told is the real reason I'm out now. I came out to stop myself listening to the mourn and keen of my own disturbing

thoughts. Trade couldn't be worse, and that's why I couldn't
pay you for that ham last night. Honest to Jasus I don't
know what's happening to the men in this town—because to
the pleasure time which as you know begins in my house
every night at eight not a soul is coming. And this is something I don't understand," she said, and fell silent. "Though
maybe it's not surprising," she said, breaking the silence,
"since I've long passed the limits where even I can with suc-
cess go on fixing up hoors to look like virgins. Of course it's
my inability to do so that's responsible for this bloodless
condition of my finances," she said. And her enormous eyes,
incessantly active, swung from us to the water of the canal
before they sprang back to Annie, who stood slender and
narrow-hipped and naked in front of her before she got into
her knickers and pulled her pinny over her head..

Nodding then, Miz Robey began to look Annie over at
close range. And, still nodding, she suddenly cupped Annie's
chin in her hand as if to confirm what she saw. "You know
you are," she said, "you're turning into quite a beaut. All I
need is you and a few like you in my cat-house and I could
shift meself into one of them squares and really clean up in
this lousy Holy Mary town."

"What do you mean—me in your cat-house?" Annie
asked.

And on the far bank the woman with the face of Lincoln was singing softly and fervently, singing to herself and
the loveliness round her.

"Nothing," Miz Robey said. "Nothing," she added.
She jerked up her head. "Later, later I might. Who knows,"
she said, and she was looking at Annie. "One day," she said.
"One day when you've stopped feeling and learned to hate a
bit. The day you realize that, for money, all things are common to humans. One day when you've discovered that in this
lousy world the end always justifies the means. Then, if—"

she paused suddenly. "Forget it," she said. "Taking you in would only be another mistake in a long, long list of mistakes, for you'd only assure the timid that whatever it was they were looking for they'd not find it in my place . . . at least, not without one shagging hell of a battle. And, bollix, you're too Goddamned innocent, anyway. Some could, but I couldn't. I haven't yet forgotten on what side of my body my heart lies. Besides, I don't want you chalked up against me. You're still only a kid, even if you have shot up some. No—let's forget that and consider instead the bevy of hoors I'm saddled with. And since it was the sport of my mad grandmother to preface all her utterings with 'Begin at home, Pet, begin at home,' we'll begin at home and we'll begin with big Moll. Now if that wan's ship of life isn't about to leave harbor, then I don't know what is. And yet, God help her, like a flower that wan was, when she first came to me—a big, white flower, glittering and quivering and offering there on the pavement the first time I ever clapped eyes on her. And look at her now! Well, whether she knows it or not she's just about come to the end of her usefulness and any day now she's going to have to wend a lonely way down to a bed in the Lock Hospital . . . Then there's Rose. Now *her* I should've left in the shoe factory I found her in, cause she's no good to me or herself. Drowsy with ignorance that girl is. And mind-sly. Gives it away. Can't raise her sight higher than a man's fly. And then there's Lena wearing herself out remembering the saints on all occasions. It's funny—I don't know what the stuff is that flows out of that hoor's heart, but it's not blood. And as for Olive—" Miz Robey broke off and in silence stared out, as if at some nightmare foe.

"What about her?" Annie asked, but Miz Robey dismissed the question.

"Okay, so you don't want to talk about Olive," Annie

said. "But about the pleasure-time—why don't you advertise?"

And back from where it was her mind had taken her,
Miz Robey said:

"Advertise?"

"Sure, the way the shops do," Annie answered, and
herself and Miz Robey were eyeing each other shrewdly.

"How advertise?" Miz Robey was trying not to appear
even interested.

"The way the shops do," Annie said again. "Write
about the pleasure-time and put it in the papers. That way
everyone would know, and come."

"That kinda thing costs plenty," Miz Robey said. "I
couldn't afford it."

"Sure you could—scour round a bit, or get a lend on
Mr. Robey."

Miz Robey shook her head. "That man is owing just
about as much as any human being can right now. Besides,
what I could raise on him ain't the kind of money I need
this Goddam awful day."

"I got a plan," Annie said, and no more.

"If it's about joining the ranks of my hoors, you can
forget it."

"It isn't, but it's worth something."

"Only if it's good." Miz Robey's eyes looked out fixed
from her painted face.

"It is," Annie, all sturdy thought now, replied.

"Enlighten us." Miz Robey settled the furs on her
shoulders, as if readying herself for yet another battle with
Annie. "So what you figure it's worth, then, this plan?"

Annie hunched her shoulders, flung her head back and
said quickly, "A quid."

"It'll have to be good," Miz Robey spoke after long
consideration.

"It's circulars," Annie said. "We get ourselves butcher paper, right? Butcher paper holds paint and is cheap if you buy in bulk. A brush, and a tin a paint: black, or maybe red. We cut the paper into squares and write on them."

Miz Robey regarded her suspiciously. "What d'you write?" Her ringed hand in her bag paused in its search and stayed still.

"All about the pleasure-time," Annie said. "Then we spread them circulars round—houses, shops, pubs. But you leave that to me and Tucker, for by the time we've finished every mother's son in Dublin will know."

"I don't want every mother's son in Dublin to know," Miz Robey said. "Just gentlemen—gentlemen with clean shirts, clean hands, and a lot of money to spend." She took her hand out of the bag, thoughtful. "How much you figure this plan of yours would cost? I mean altogether?"

Annie calculated quickly: "Paint, a dollar. Brush—say half. Paper—twelve and six the lot," she said.

A contemplative look settled over Miz Robey's face, then the slow, big smile she gave when she wanted something for nothing, or was about to cheat you.

"You said a quid for the plan, right? So I'll tell you: you go get that stuff, but instead of paying you in bits I'll settle up for the lot tomorrow. No, listen," she cried, rebutting Annie's cynical laugh, "you write out all them particulars, hand them circulars round like you said, and I'll give you an extra quid. How's that? For the complete job, two pound twelve and six, plus the ten bob for the ham. I promise."

"Agreed," Annie said. "But I want no trouble, mind. Because I need that money bad. Next week I start dealing and—" She broke off as Miz Robey opened her mouth and made the sign of the cross.

"Ah, Annie, as if I'd break a promise, knowing the

way you feel about them, or let either of youse down when
I know how important it is to youse."

"Okay, okay," Annie said. "But let's get this clear:
a quid for the plan—the quid you promised—twelve and
six for the material—ten bob for the ham—plus ten bob
delivery charges—right?" She had added ten shillings not
included in the original terms. I waited for Robey to spot
the difference and object, but she didn't. All she did was
smile big and head for home.

"Now tell us where we get the stuff," I said.

"Woolworths." Annie grinned. "We haven't been there
for a long time and that floorwalker must be missing us."
And later: "You cut and print one," she said, "and I'll copy
from that." And she did, using up what was left of the day
in Miz Robey's red hall doing so.

On Saturday morning we returned to the task again,
with me cutting while Annie with care and delicate concen-
tration copied and wrote in red paint, using capital letters
with flourishes under each line. "MEN," she wrote, "WEL-
COMED TO THE PLEASURE-TIME." "AT 8." "AT MRS. ROBEY'S."
And underneath she put the address.

"Lovely," Miz Robey said the circulars were, just as
we were finishing off the last lot. And they were, till Big
Moll put her big mouth in and ruined everything.

"But for Christ's sake, what are them men being
welcomed to—a jumble sale?" She came, a young woman
dressed up in the body of an old one, down the stairs, and
stood with Olive, Rose, Margo, and Lena over us in the
hall papered in a color that had once been crimson but was
now faded into a strange richness of hues, like a garden
filled with dying roses. In the dim light, the walls blushed
and gleamed in places, the way the paint on the faces bending over us did.

"Them," Big Moll said, and she meant the circulars,
"should have something about us on them."

"What do you mean, something about youse on them?"
Annie's eyes, which while she worked had been dark and
gentle, flashed fury at the disparagement roughing Big
Moll's voice.

"Things." Big Moll, ragged and moving, showed her
thighs through the flimsy pink of a wrap-over that trailed.
"Things," she said again, and looked down at us with
watery eyes that were pale and blue, rimmed with feverish
red and sleepless black. "Things about girls or hoors, or
whatever the hell it is you want to call us. And sex. They
should definitely say something about sex, for it's certain we
don't want no craw-thumping bastards with gumdrops where
their balls should be coming here to do the stations of the
cross. This in case youse don't know it is a cat-house, and
not some shagging Legion of Mary hostel."

"That's for sure," Rose said.

"That's true," Miz Robey added.

"So what'll I do?" Annie asked.

"Put down something about my nine different posi-
tions," Rose said, and winked.

"She could an all," Miz Robey said. She looked at
Rose. "And while she's at it, she could, if she had any sense,
tell you a wise hoor would reserve eight a them for the more
solemn moments of her life. Last night you nearly brought
the ceiling down, going through they all for that little puke-
faced solicitor. Why don't you tell that constipated ruin of
a man you're athletically minded and leave it at that? And
Olive—from now on a little less of the port that pours
purple—and no more lectures on the state of Ireland for
that wog waiter from the Shelbourne."

"But that bastard thinks he's Napoleon," Olive cried.

"All Frenchmen do, but that's no excuse for you sounding off like a Republican drowning in a sea of Imperialism.
And Margo, stop setting your mind at targets above the
waist. You're too old to play at indignation while reality

squats outside your door spitting venom through the key-
hole. And Lena—was it laughing you were on the landing
at five this morning, or just clearing your throat? And who
was it standing at the foot of them stairs, threatening us all
with Catholic action?"

"The vet from Richmond Street," Lena said, and gig-
gled, and fluttered in her gray tulle like a gentle ghost
haunting the wreckage of an empty house—and about to
say something else, Miz Robey changed her mind and looked
down at us.

"I have a feeling these circulars are going to be the
last of my enthusiasms," she said.

"So what'll I write then?" Annie asked.

"Just put down 'GIRLS,' " I said, "and see how it looks.
Put it down in blocks," I added.

"Put down pricks in blocks and see how they look,"
Rose snapped, her glance fast on Miz Robey while Annie
knelt silent, thinking out this new demand.

"Just put down 'GIRLS,' " I whispered; and she did, and
without help, except with the spelling.

She showed the first sample to Big Moll, who, some-
what pacified, gave a grudging snort.

"See," Annie said. "That should take the hump off
your shoulders and the look of heart strain off your face.
For now it begins with men and ends with girls."

"If I didn't know better I'd say you were a stranger to
life," Big Moll said. She looked at Annie. "Still, maybe it'll
work. Maybe. I just hope to Christ it does," she said, and
across her mouth was a quick, red slash of paint, and jutting
from it a cigarette butt with a red-hot coal at the end of it.

"So do I," Annie replied as Margo, looking like Mr.
Cribbens' picture of Brittania without her trident, steered
the others back up the stairs in front of her.

"From the moithering dusk and the fugitive play of

children and lovers they go," Miz Robey said. "It's a natural instinct," she added, as Annie's glance followed them up to the first landing, stacked with ferns in pots, then sweeping over Miz Robey, fell critically to the stack of papers to which "GIRLS" in blocks had yet to be added. Taking it in turn to print, we worked quickly—while Miz Robey talked about how she would have to return to the struggle to give up drink, and then about how the first house she was ever in was in Munich in a sidestreet stuck between a synagogue and a clinic for expectant mothers—and all the time watching Annie spell out "GIRLS" over and over, and sipping the drink in her hand and finishing it just as we got to our feet with the circulars that was to bring every man in Dublin running to her door.

"So the work's done. Finished," Annie said. "You pay us now."

Miz Robey looked down at her feet, slowly and carefully drew them together, and finally rose to them swaying a little as she did so.

"So for the shoddiness of needs are shoes made out of last year's hide," she said. She looked at Annie. "There was a time when men found my palaver a lovely addition to the rest of me. But in the heel of the hunt I think the truth is best and the truth is, the older I get the less able I am to face calamity—but pay you now is something I cannot do," she said, and she said it formal. "But," she went on—and she stressed the "but"—"I shall settle my account with you as promised *after* you have completed the job and delivered them circulars."

Annie drew in her breath and gave me a strong quick glance; then together we focused the full battering ram of our gaze on her. "Ah, for Christ's sake!" she cried, and her voice in the hall's silence fought off our stares.

"Down there," she said, pointing to the floor, "is a

basement, and is what in any Christian country would be called not holy ground but sacred ground, is it not?" She waited and we let her, and I knew if she thought tears a solution she'd use them. "So tell me? Would I make a promise standing here on the very relics of that man's skeleton and not honor it? Would I?"

"Not much you wouldn't," Annie sneered.

"Ah, Annie . . . ." Miz Robey's eyelids closed heavy as her face collapsed in utter sadness. "Am I not," she cried suddenly, "only hard on hoors and ponces and generous to the poor? . . . Am I not, dear God, only . . ." Her eyes opening, flew from me to Annie.

"Ah, Annie, you gotta trust me. You gotta stop thinking everyone you meet is out to do you."

"They are an all," Annie snapped.

"Ah . . . but not me," Miz Robey said. "Would I add to the troubled throb of your heart at a time like this? And you, God help you, fending off that many-handed mother of yours and that factory." She paused. "You must trust somebody, Annie. Trust me. . . ." And somehow, and before we rightly knew what she was up to, she had worked us the length of the hall to the door, had opened it, and had us through it.

"When youse come back, every penny of that money will be waiting for youse."

"It better be," Annie said, and her gaze was split level, but Miz Robey had already closed the door.

"What's the bet," Annie said as we lugged the armfuls of circulars over the bridge into Ranalagh, "that she'll offer to let's hold Mr. Robey instead of paying us? Or give us a cup of tea in the parlor."

"She wouldn't," I said, "she knows we're depending on that money."

"Wouldn't she?!" Annie asked. "That wan would

chance her arm at anything, only this time she'll be making one big hell of a mistake. Because I don't want to hold Mr. Robey in my arms any more. That's kid stuff. And neither do I want to sit in no parlor of no cat-house listening to her going on about the oul head that blithely bore the burden of the purple biretta, not being what it was."

"Or about how thoroughly un-national she's always been, and how by running houses abroad she's impeded Ireland's progress," I said, and filled with an assurance that was hardly my own, I added: "But we won't be asked."

We left the Ranalagh Road and turned into North-brook and, avoiding only the Hogans' house, left a circular at every other; and hours later returned to Rock Street to leave what was left in the pubs and the shops along it, and then made for Miz Robey's. We saw one man go and another come, just as we reached the steps, and at the door saw Miz Robey with her big smile greeting the newcomer. Waiting till he'd gone in, we then darted up the steps. For although she'd seen us, Miz Robey had been about to close the door. I heard her sigh, just as Annie shouted: "Hold it!" and in her sigh heard the answer to all Annie's suspicions.

"I can't pay you," Miz Robey said, without any pream-ble. "I just can't. The bastards are going this evening like Dali Lamas from the pleasures of the body. So I'll just have to owe it to youse."

"Oh no," Annie cried, and her breath fell stubborn, thicker, faster. "You'll pay us now. And while I'm at it, you better understand we're not looking for something for noth-ing. What we want is money for work done. You pay us now. You promised."

"You gotta give me time." Miz Robey narrowed the slit the door was making.

"I don't have time," Annie cried, shoving herself against it.

And she didn't, for with only a week to go before
Barker's opened its doors, time for Annie was shrinking
at a nightmare rate.

"Well, you'll just have to make time, then, won't you?"
Miz Robey snapped.

Annie shook her head. "I must have that money tonight."

"Well, you can't," Miz Robey said, and looked over
her shoulder in the direction of voices raised.

"But you promised," Annie, against the door, looked
like a wing-clipped bird fluttering.

"Promised! Promised!" Miz Robey roared. "You and
your shagging promises! Jasus, I've never known a child like
you." And then, on a swift and sudden change of mood and
tactics, she smiled. "I'll tell you what—" she began. "Supposing I—" But she got no further.

"No! No!" Annie shouted. "You're not palming me
off with Mr. Robey. We want to be paid."

"Okay, okay—no need to bring the whole lousy street
running to my door," Miz Robey cried. "And no need at
all to get yourself riz. And if that's how you're going to
carry on over my financial embarrassment, that's only tem-
porary, mind, then I'll shift change with neither of youse
any longer. And there was I," she added on a sigh, "thinking we were friends. But then I'm not the first woman to
end up with stones in her hands that she took to be jewels,
and I daresay I won't be the last."

And, with that, Miz Robey slammed the door on us.

8

The evening had streaked into the rowdy exhilaration of night in Rock Street. Round us when we let them, kids bulky with impudence tore. On either side of the street, in the dark ruins of halls from which doors had been ripped in some long and bitter winter, women—bibbed, overalled, shawled, and bloused—stood. Below them on the wrecked steps of tenements, others sat mouthing beside tidy-limbed girls with just-washed hair drenched in paraffin poured from cans and then, with long, unbroken strokes, fine-combed for nits. Above them, in open windows, men shirtless leaned, and beside them women half naked, in bits of slips, roared down to others thinking about tomorrow's bread as they searched for bargains among the dealers' stalls and at the same time nursed babies fisting breasts and nipples that showed black in the dark.

Through the rasping, frosted glass of the pubs, lights flared, and when a door opened, singing and shouts shot a welcome to all that passed. A young girl in a crimson blaze

125

of cheap silk went off with her fella to her first dance, and from a lamppost Carmel Mac, on her own and looking smug, swung on a yellow penny straw off an orange box; and at the mouth of Ellen Simms' lane, Johnny Roscoe and a gang of men stood in a warm-smelling mist over a game of toss and, like money-lenders or monks at prayer, sent out sharp, questioning looks to anyone who came near.

Going down the street to the Green and the grand streets off it, bloated blossom-faced whores like Lilly Sherman sidestepped others sidling up it, most of them hugging bottles of red biddy in a rigor-mortis clutch under flung coats, and all of them, like one-armed Hop-the-Twig, bewildered from being bullied into too long a life as they made for the consoling dark of the canal and the shelter of elders and willows, and the randy, lusty men waiting under them.

From Telfords the organ-makers, an organ thundered over the clang of trams that gushed sparks and slowed, the way Ellen Simms did, just before they took the bridge, and as they passed the children's hospital where the child Annie had buried had died of the croup. Directly opposite us, the widow went with weeds flying under the strangled splutter of gaslight greening ghostly her prowlike face—and in the swept, lit, and open door of his shop, Mr. Doyle, convent-neat and jet-black, sent over quick, cross-grained looks at us, while a few yards away on our right, Mr. Cribbens, hatted and war-medaled and wearing a large red buttonhole, stood drunk-sodden in the door of his, and sang mouldy a song to which, on the path in front of him, his wife and slob of a son and two daughters marched.

On the wide spread of Miz Robey's steps, Annie, in smoldering fury, sat with her back to the door that had been slammed in our faces. The biggest building in Rock Street, Miz Robey's whorehouse was five stories high, with four

windows across every one of them, blinded by lace backed
by yards of claret-colored stuff·you couldn't see through.
The door, once a Kelly green, was now faded and smeared
with patches made by the snow, wind, and rain of many seasons. Flanking it on one side, railings guarded the basement
that wasn't lived in, but used as a kind of chapel, where the
casket that held the ashes of the late Mr. Robey was kept.
It was toward this and the faces obscure and clotting at
corners along the street that my mind was straying when
Annie, sounding briar-sharp and as if somebody had contradicted her, said suddenly:

"I *should've known*. I just should've, only I never
thought she'd try her tricks over an important thing like
this.

"I mean, I know she did us over the ham and I know
Robey must be about the biggest bester ever to hit this
street, but I just never, ever believed she could stoop so low.
Before, I've never much minded her attempts at wiping my
eye or conning me out of a copper, though I always let on
and acted up when she did. But this is a different thing altogether. This time I was neither buying, selling, or swapping.
This was supposed to be payment for work done—two days'
work, for that's what it took the pair of us to make, print,
and deliver them circulars. Two whole days. All of yesterday and all of today. And what have we got to show for it?
Nothing."

"Plus nothing," I said, and I added: "We even missed
out on the bens."

"I know," she replied quickly. "Because I was convinced the work we were doing for Robey would be much
more profitable. And it would've, if she'd been honest and
decent and kept her word."

"It would've bought us the cart, in case Ellen Simms
does change her mind about giving us hers," I said.

Annie nodded. "*And* left us with something to hand up at home," she said. "Instead of which, we're sitting here like paupers on a Saturday night, and with only one more week to go before Barker's opens its doors and I have to direct my feet through them."

Annie paused, and across the street Mr. Doyle left the door of his shop and walked out to the edge of the path.

Holding up in his right hand one of the circulars we had left with him, he waved it like a banner, then, taking it in both hands, he tore it to shreds and with a flourish of courage flung the pieces in our direction.

"That man's lucky he has the street between us," Annie said.

"What are we going to do?" I asked.

"About him?" Annie glared across at Mr. Doyle.

"No, about Robey," I said.

Annie shook her head. "I don't know. But I'm thinking," she said, as Mr. Doyle, still with his gaze fixed on us, stepped back into the door of his shop. A bunch of kids came up and the more brazen tried to sit on the steps beside us. At first Annie just looked at them. Then one of them asked her if it was cold up there. She made a grab for the one nearest her but he ducked and ran. I watched them go— we both did—and then I said:

"What are we going to do?"

Annie shook her head. "I don't know yet, but something, for I want that cart, or the price of one, too bad to be tricked out of it by Miz Robey."

Then suddenly she jumped to her feet, stood for a moment as if on the wave of some terrible dilemma, then went over to the railings.

"C'mon," she said, and across the street Mr. Doyle in his door was still watching us.

"Where are we going?" I said.

"Down into that basement, to get the only thing that oul bitch cares about," Annie said. "And this time," she added, "*I'll* hold onto them man's ashes the way the dealers do, till she does pay us."

"But the dealers *don't* hold onto them ashes," I said, as we went over the railings, down into the basement.

"So they don't," Annie admitted as we raised the window with the broken latch and slipped into the room. "But I will. Maybe God did make me and Miz Robey, but if He did he matched us."

"She's never let them ashes outa this house," I said as we groped our way across the room. "In fact, she's never even let us see them," I added, and finding the switch for the light flooded the room with it.

The yellowing walls had shadows on them, where pictures and furniture had been. There was a stove, never used, and in front of it a table covered with a white cloth. There were two long, slender, twin-branched brass candlesticks; and between them the mahogany brass-trimmed, claw-footed casket rested.

It might be locked, I thought, half hoping it would be. But it wasn't.

Annie lifted the casket, raising it the way the priest does the monstrance at benediction. Gently, she swung the lid up, and as she did so a sweet, musty smell filled the room. We looked into the casket, its undeniable source. It's what happens when people are burnt, I thought, and saw Annie go to stir with her finger the funeral pile.

"No," I said, and shivered.

"Why not?"

But I didn't know why. I saw her scoop with her hand, and as she did so a garden smell, dated from summers past, rose into our nostrils.

"This isn't ash," she said, and overhead a board

creaked and a foot trod quiet, so as not to disturb further the exposed dream.

"What is it?" I whispered.

"Rose petals. Dried rose petals!" Annie's eyes widened.

"Are you sure?"

"Positive." She looked at me.

"Maybe certain people change into rose petals when they die."

"Only saints, if them," Annie replied. "And Mr. Robey—he was no saint—we'd've heard—that is, if there ever was a . . ." Her voice, loaded with doubt, fell away, but I had followed her thoughts.

"The cheat," I said.

"She's worse." Annie carefully closed the lid. "Robey's a liar," she said, and her face narrowed with thought.

"And all this time—" I began, and in the room the silence I fell into swung backward and forward, waiting for the moment to strike.

"C'mon," Annie said.

"You can't take that." I pointed to the casket.

"It's not locked or nailed down," Annie said. "And even if it was, I'd like someone to make the mistake of trying to stop me."

We left the room, and back up on the street again Annie went up the steps and banged on the green hall door, opened as always by Miz Robey. She stood, smiling the big, gold smile. And not smiling, but looking the way people do waiting for the aching shapes of winter to dissolve into a more familiar road and street.

And then she grabbed, and Annie was rising out of her reach.

"Wait," Annie cried, "till I tell you about them kids who broke into your kitchen and fecked Mr. Robey."

Miz Robey stood rigid.

"Heathens," she said. "Heathens!" she screamed, and people passing looked and went on. "Give me that." She tried to reach, but Annie stepped back.

"After. After you've settled with us," she said, and against her chest she hugged the casket tight.

Recovering, Miz Robey flung the hall door wide, but Annie, rejecting the invitation, shook her head, and Miz Robey went and came back, waving two pound-notes.

"You owe us three," Annie said. "Plus twelve and six."

"It's all I've got." Miz Robey held the money out.

Annie hesitated, but then—to my surprise—the exchange was made.

"He's safe," she said.

"You looked?" Miz Robey could not resist.

"We looked," Annie said. "And he smelled good—real good." Her gaze, unflinching, met Miz Robey's.

"Gentlemen," Miz Robey said, "always do." And the grimace her lips had shaped themselves into began the slow, big, golden smile. She looked hard at Annie then, as if seeking something beyond the blank innocence, and, not finding it, shook her head. "I thank you," she said, in control and very much the lady again. "And *Mister* Robey thanks you." And, pushing up her head, she added: "And now what's left of my buxom loveliness must be queenly cloaked—so if you kids don't mind, I got company."

"But Mr. Robey isn't in that casket," I said as the door closed. "They weren't even his ashes. And why would she want rose petals?"

"She doesn't," Annie said. "It's something else."

"Like what? And why didn't you tell her?"

"I was about to, but then I couldn't. I know Robey's a cheat and a liar, but she's not like us. If she knew we knew for sure, it would take the heart out of her, and she'd never be uppity again, or pull the lady of the manor on us, the way she does. She's not ordinary—but then, there's enough ordinary people cluttering up this world as it is. And if she knew we knew what is in that casket, she'd think we'd tell, then everyone would know." Annie paused and looked at me. "You don't believe God's all around us, do you? But you let on you do."

"Only to please my mother."

"See," Annie pounced. "And it makes Robey different, having them ashes. After all, even the commonalty could have rose petals."

"But she hasn't got ashes," I protested.

"Agreed," Annie grinned. "But who but her and us know?" She faced me. "Nobody. Because we won't tell."

And, although I didn't know we wouldn't then, we never did.

"She still owes us one pound twelve and six," I said.

"She does indeed, but that two quid will do nicely to be going on with," someone said, and Mrs. Murphy, with her hair streeling over the shoulders of the coat flung round her, was pushing herself up the steps, with her hands stretched toward us.

9

When we began the second round of the last Sunday supper we were ever to have with Ellen Simms, it was seven o'clock. The time of evening when in the old days we'd've been out gathering from the rooms round the lanes and street the swill we sold to Mr. Cullen at twopence a bucket for his pigs. Or on business bent scouring the tree-lined roads edging the city or with foxy caution prowling the hedge-lined ones beyond it. Or running—in search of something of worth through Sunday's bells and sleepy Te Deums, the green-shuttered streets battered senseless under the fisted thump of organ and Sabbath dinners rumbling narky summonses to a remembered bearded benevolence.

Or on a night like this crammed with people out in shiny only-worn-on-Sunday-clothes, rank with the smell of camphor, cabbage smoke, and coddle—swimming in the slow water of the canal—or jeering the clumsy efforts of a lock-keeper forking out the bloated body of a man or woman floating face down among the swishy reeds, tangled ferns, and seamy shade of slimy mosses. Or we might've been robbing turf boats between bridges or sitting in crowded loneliness with my mother on the Rock Street side of the canal, listening to her shape up a Virgin Mary world in which we didn't believe but which according to her was sane and round and just and reasonable—and from which for her the colors of all that was good in life had not yet faded—or in silence mulling over our own, a mixture of good and bad, of collision between belief and disbelief, and filled always with faces and minds furrowed with heaven's venoms against ill things done.

Or we might just've been listening to the click of the steel knitting needles in her hands as she explained in detail to Annie, in a fit of wanting to know how to knit, how to turn the heel of a sock—or as she coaxed into longer life with a needle and thread a pair of trousers belonging to me, or a coat or dress off one of the others—listening to her talk when asked about the ferny place from which she had come and which Annie called "the countryland," and about which in a quiet or pensive mood she liked to hear.

Or away from my mother's gentle nature we could've been on the other side of the canal with the Poet and his doubting strenuous one—watching him between coughs dip into the newspaper cone of Passion Rousers we were feeding him. But this was a different evening. We were not on the canal with the Poet, listening to him pondering whether or not annihilation's waste would be his when the end came—neither were we skimming the fields of Milltown or streeling the banks of the Dodder while Annie, judging the works of God and man, set out in clear strong terms how she could've improved on them, and I stared up at the sky patched with red and strident green and made patterns with the shapes of rooks scattering across them like souls afraid of heaven.

Instead tonight, chained fast to where the new Annie wanted to be, we were eating supper with Ellen Simms in her room in Galleons Lane. It was a late supper, this last meal that the three of us would ever eat together at Ellen Simms' big kitchen table. And on it on plates in front of us, marble-headed scallions veined with green gleamed on large leaves of fresh salad. Beside them pink slices of cold corned beef lay; and on little plates sucking up to the ones we were eating from, huge cuts of homemade brown bread sat, soaked and lathered under salt butter melting.

Starting in on second helpings and passing the dishes back and forth among ourselves, we were not talking about the subjects we usually thought about with Ellen Simms, and so far no mention at all had been made of the thing that had brought us to her door tonight. Instead there began a strange conversation that was finally to lead Ellen Simms into telling us a story we had never heard before, and neither had anybody else. And it came about in this way:

"I was saying," Annie said, "that nothing is ever what you think it will be. I mean, a person can't get up in the morning and be sure that this thing or that thing will happen that day. I mean you couldn't bet your life on a certain thing happening, could you? I don't rightly know how to explain what I mean," she said; and right away she began to try to tell Ellen Simms about the things that had gone wrong for us in the past two weeks.

About Maggie Hyland and the fight with the beggars. About the way I had lost my hat and coat to them. About the stuff lifted from Mick O'Brien's, and about how we had not made a single penny on it. About the work done for Miz Robey and how we had lost to her mother the two pounds

Robey had given us, and about the three shillings she had
had to insist on her mother giving me. And as she talked
she stopped now and then to find the right word to tell of
doubts in herself she had not felt before, and to see if Ellen
Simms was following her.

"For instance," she said, looking straight at Ellen
Simms, "I used to think till you told me otherwise that
everything was the same all over. I used to think that
every country in the world was the same, with the same
food, the same money, and the same people. But it isn't
like that at all, is it? In fact, if I'm to believe you and them
books up there on them shelves, nothing at all is the way
I imagined it was. Every country is different and every single
person in that country is different. In the same way you, me,
and Tucker is different. Understand?" She paused and
looked at me, and then at Ellen Simms, who gave her a long
uncomprehending stare.

"Okay, then, *I'll* tell you what I mean," she said. "For
instance, I know you're a dealer—right. But if some stranger
was to come through that door right now and we were to
ask him to tell us what you were, I bet he wouldn't be able
to. At least, not just by looking. Because indoors and without your shawl you don't look like a dealer. And neither do
you act like one. In the first place every other dealer that
I know keeps what they don't sell on a Saturday night under
their beds till Monday morning. Then if it's cabbage or anything perishable, all they do is tear off the withered leaves
and give what's left a quick hose-down under the pipe, then
set it back up for sale again. But you never do. You never
keep anything under your bed, or in the house overnight,
and if you are left with stuff on your hands, either you sell it
cheap or give it away for nothing. Also you can read and
write. And you're neat always and you never go on the drink
the way most of them do.

"And then of course there's this room and that crib,"
Annie said, and pausing, her glance flew to a cabinet set
between two windows on which the nativity scene was set
out. "Well, nobody lives with bare whitewashed walls and
nobody expects to come across a crib right in the middle of
the month of August," she said, and her glance, straying
back again to the crib, went over the little figures carved in
wood and brightly painted: Jesus in his straw-lined crib,
Mary, Joseph, the Ox, the Ass, the Wise Men, the Shepherds, and the Angel. And behind them larger angels holding up crowns of red candles and with flowers in their yellow
hair. "Not that I've anything against bare walls, or a crib
in August," Annie said. "It's just that it's unexpected. It's
just that I don't know anyone else who lives without a picture of some sort on the wall, and I've certainly never known
anybody who left a crib out from one year's end to the other.
Tucker's mother doesn't," she said; and under her bitter
black brows, Ellen Simms' caverned brown eyes glittered
smoky. "I'm not criticizing," Annie said, "it's just that it's
unexpected, and somehow I never allow for the unexpected
or take it into account."

She paused and leaned both elbows on the table, and
I waited for Ellen Simms to tell her to remove them the
way she sometimes did; but she didn't. Instead she pushed
away her plate and, easing back on her chair, reached into
the pocket of the blue cotton apron she wore indoors and
took out a clay pipe, a box of matches, and a brown tobacco
pouch, and set them out on the table in front of her. In her
fifties, Ellen Simms was still youthful-looking, with her slim
hard body and her general appearance still handsome. Her
hair, drawn back into a low thick bun on the nape of her
neck, was still jet-black and her well-molded lips set in a
firm skin, brownish white. Never beautiful, she nevertheless
gave an impression of beauty. A hard dark violent beauty,

opaque as stone and almost as inhuman. Like a dead tree on a lonely road she was, I was thinking, when Annie, looking at me, said suddenly: "Unexpected, isn't it?"

"What is?" I asked.

"Seeing a crib in August."

I nodded agreement and thought about my mother, who like Ellen Simms also took care of things, but who instead of leaving our crib out all year round brought ours out only at Christmas so that the pleasure was always new.

And she had other rituals too; and as Annie picked up a scallion and bit into the head, I remembered the drink my mother made from hops every June, and the head and face she carved out of a turnip at Halloween, and the paper chains she made and garlanded the ceiling with on Christmas Eve. Also, unlike Ellen Simms who lived and liked living with bare walls with the bricks showing, my mother fresh-papered the walls and whitewashed the ceilings of our two rooms every spring, and it was from things like this that the year for me gained shape and the rhythm I wanted my life to have.

"Of course, it's not taking the unexpected into account that's my trouble," Annie said; and she watched Ellen Simms twist off a ragged fringe of tobacco from the blackened bowl of her pipe, and then, with her left hand which had been stiffened by a winter rheumatism, stuff it back down again. "I mean," Annie said, "it's like when I come here and see that crib. I know I'll see it, but just the same, every time I do I get a shock. It's like that pack of beggars stripping Tucker of that hat and coat," she said, as Ellen Simms struck a match, and without shifting her somber gaze off Annie, held the match close over the bowl of her pipe and sucked. "Now that was unexpected and had never happened to us before," Annie said into the blue spiral of smoke that rose and hung in folding and unfolding layers over us and the table. "And for God's sake who'd've thought there was

one among that pack with the courage to do such a thing?"
she asked, and looking through the smoke at Ellen Simms,
added, "And it was unexpected the way you said nothing
about it.

"I was sure you'd give us a hard time over that, and
so was Tucker. He even thought you might change your
mind about giving us your cart on account of it." Annie
paused, and I glanced at Ellen Simms and tried to read her,
but she remained impassive, thoughtful silent.

"Then last night," Annie said, "my Ma grabbing that
money from us before my hand could even feel the strength
of it. What I'm really trying to say is I just never allowed
for none of them things taking place when I threw up the
milk rout and talked Tucker into quitting Mr. Cribbens.
Even though I know that man was a robber an all. I thought
everything would go as I planned. With us doing the bens
and making all we could on the sale of the cinders. After all,
I was only asking for things to stay the way they always had
till you quit dealing and until we began. But now . . ." Her
voice broke and she looked up at the ceiling.

"But now?" Ellen Simms asked, and into the pause that
came she sat up straight on her chair and her lips and
square white teeth clamped down hard on the stem of the
pipe in her mouth. Annie shook her head, and I guessed
that with her now it was more a matter of feelings than of
facts or words she was finding it difficult to explain.

"I feel bunched," she said finally. And the sounds in
the room and outside in the lane were mingled, and in the
summer evening long drawn. Her glance roped in me and
Ellen Simms and the room. "I feel suddenly bet," she said.
"Like I've lost the full use of my head or something. I
mean . . ." She started again, but Ellen Simms cut her short.

"I know what you mean," she said. "But you can't
afford to feel bunched or bet."

"Maybe not, but I do just the same, with the way

things have been going," Annie said. "I'm sick at the very sameness of the days because lately every single day is filled with downright bad luck or with things just going contrary. And yet," she added and paused, "at the same time everything is changing, if you know what I mean."

"I know what you mean," Ellen Simms said, and the smoke from her pipe was beginning to lie bitter and warm and stagnant in the room. "I also know there's just no such thing as sameness," she said. "It just looks that way sometimes."

"How do you mean?" Annie asked.

"What I say," Ellen Simms said. "Maybe we do the same things every day and even go back over the same ground. And perhaps we may even have the same contentious, vexing, and sad-making thoughts, but inside where you can't see them, things are changing all the time—working themselves up into a state where they all come together like peas in a pod and finally show. Then before you know where you are you're saying something's happened and your life is so different you can't believe it's your own."

"Yes, that's it," Annie said when Ellen Simms paused and let her hand with the pipe in it rest on the edge of the table. "One day everything is in full control," she said. "You know or think you do, where it is you're going, and why, and what it is you'll see when you get there. Then without as much as a by-your-leave, everything you had all neatly tied up is gone and you're left staring at Jesus only knows what. Only it's never at what you know or are used to, or want, and right away you're stranded in a misery that was none of your making. Or you think it wasn't. But that's only because you haven't been aware of the changes taking place inside yourself. So when something does happen, the old you is gone, and what's left can't handle or cope with the event. So you feel bunched. Bet. But we wouldn't feel either if we had been aware of the changes going on in the first place, and in spite of them held something of the old self in reserve. It's only when we forget and let go the thing from which we draw our strength that we leave ourselves defenseless."

"That's when the hard knocks come. The ones that do the real damage. And they come always from where we least expect them. It was like that with me," Ellen Simms said and, pausing, looked over in silence through the darkening room to the windows and the coarse white lace curtains that had been pushed aside—to the cabinet between the windows and the nativity scene; and from that she looked to her bed in the corner, with its polar-white fringed quilt against the bare whitewashed wall, and over it and running the length of it the four unpainted shelves she had put up herself to hold her books. "Thirty years ago," she said suddenly: and now, sharp, suspicious, watchful, imperious, and implacable, *she was a dealer* and looked the way she did in the street, as she began the story we had never heard before. The story of herself and Andy Prince.

"I was twenty-three," she said. "I had a hard-scrubbed face and chopped hair. My mother was dead. Died when I was a child. I lived in a lane like yours. Along with thirty-six other families. There was a pump in the middle of the lane and behind it three lavatories for one hundred and sixty people. We had rats in the houses and strife that grew out of the walls of them. I lived with my father and his bothered widowed sister. She had teeth like cloves and black hair she could sit on. But she wore it looped over ears pierced for rings that dropped in heavy solid gold to her shoulders.

"She suffered from chronic indigestion and a voice that complained. Often. And always about me to my father. In his bare feet that man stood seven foot high. He wore boots. Heavy hobnailers. He owned a horse fit only for the

knackers and a dray. Worked building sites and neither
smoke nor drank. I looked after the two rooms we had
because my aunt was never well enough to do more than the
rosary. I also took care of the horse. Harnessing him up in
the morning and unharnessing him again at night. I fed and
watered him and cleaned his stable. And in between I was
kicked. It's almost all I can remember about my father. I've
tried hard since, but I can never remember that man giving
me as much as a passing nod of approval. All I remember
is the kicks. He used to place the toecap of his right boot in
the small of my back. Never anywhere else; and never once
did he miss.

"His aim was always accurate. Should've been a foot-
baller that man. But you grow tired of pain. I did, and one
day I left and went where I wanted to be. To a room on my
own in a house over on the north strand. For the first time
in my life I felt human. And I was happy. And knew it. That
was the thing about it. I was happy and I knew it. Most of
us don't, you know, even when we are; but I did. I had a
job—a good one in a shop in Grafton Street. Dealt in
sweets, cigarettes, birthday cards, and fruit out of season.
I was there two years. Then just before the Christmas of
the second, I was in O'Connell Street one afternoon waiting
to cross and looking at the lights and the people crowding in
and out of the shops through flurries of snow.

"It was about four. Dark enough for caution. And I
was waiting to cross the street. Waiting for a crowd of
soldiers on horses to pass. Lovely animals creating an uproar
you could hear a mile away. Like drums the hooves of them
horses were. Drums beating deep . . . and frisky, a lot of
them. Sauntering past demons, shying at shadows. A few
acting flash. Tossing metal. It was the horses I was watching when I was asked my name. By a soldier on one of them,
bent over. I didn't answer at all, for I could see the man

asking was the kind who'd never have to struggle through
the alphabet to answer a short letter. Besides I wasn't the
kind, my aunt used to say. I never would be. And between her
and my father, I wasn't. I will tell you the truth, my aunt
used to say; and she did. The result was that at twenty-three
I couldn't say the things men wanted to hear. I couldn't lie,
or flatter either a man's vanity or his strength."

Ellen Simms paused abruptly and her glance, brooding
in the trough of the sudden silence, excluded me and fell on
Annie and stayed, as if she wanted to communicate to her
alone, something other than the story she was telling. I
watched her dark face struggle to open, and then saw it
close again as she withdrew whatever it was she had been
about to offer. "Anyway," she said, breaking the silence
while I continued to stare at the dark square of face before
us, "when I saw the fair looks of the fella asking I knew
things must always be easy for him. And I thought, why
should they be. Sometimes, I thought to myself, they should
be different, even for him.

"So, composing myself to resist, I heard him asking
again, and let him ask till the horse he was on gave up fighting the reins—quivered like St. Vitus and came close, drench-
ing me and all about me in a stream of sweat. 'I'll not stir
till you tell me,' the fella on it said, and bent down toward
me over the pommel. So I told him, blazing my own impudence up at the blue eyes, just as the horse under him began
to prance.

" 'I'll see you so,' he said then; and he said when, and
he said where, and cantered off. I watched him, and now
he'd gone I could with calm eyes. Because for a minute, and
while he was beside me, I'd been put off course. And . . ."
Annie's prompt broke into the pause that ticked with the
alarm clock between the china twin dogs on the mantelpiece.

"Did you?" Annie asked, and added, "turn up, I mean."

Ellen Simms nodded. "I did. But awkwardly, and needing help," she said. "In the main door of the General Post Office the following night. He was the first person I'd ever known who couldn't look at me enough. I could feel the blast of that fella's eyes on me the whole night. It was strange, because my father's eyes used to stream off into long and lonely distances at the sight of me. But Andy Prince's eyes stayed.

"We were married before Christmas. The week before. That crib was the first thing he ever gave me. Bought it off a dealer's stall in Moore Street."

"I never knew you'd been married," Annie said when Ellen Simms stopped speaking, and it seemed as if she had forgotten us or was not going to tell us more.

"For five years. For five years," Ellen Simms said with unshakable certainty. And then began the story of those years. Of her and Andy Prince. And the story went from that first meeting in the snow in O'Connell Street to the sit-down supper for thirty invited relatives and guests that Andy Prince's brother gave for them on the family's farm in Limerick. And then to the wedding at the church in Aungier Street. The honeymoon in the west in a cottage on a stretch of the coast between Galway and Roundstone.

Then Dublin again and the house beside the Phoenix Park near the barracks where Andy Prince was stationed. And the days then merging one into another, and the weeks, the months, the years together. To the fifth and leaves turning, and the trees and the grass in the park where they sometimes walked, smoky and autumn gray and gold. And the baby begun. Big with the future she bought a dress. A proud red dress. The waiting then, and the knitting, the sewing; and in between Ellen Simms taking good care of Andy Prince—pressing his uniform and cleaning with Brasso the brass buttons on it—and cleaning the boots with polish and the ox-blood colored leggings that were best done with milk.

Through the darkness of the ember days to flowers,
yellow, wind-tossed under the sometimes drained sky, and
the baby pink of the flowering cherry. The new spring, and
inside her the baby with a life and rhythm all its own. Till
for no reason, fear came. Not a creeping Jesus kind, but a
sudden growing anxiety that something was on its way that
would jelly the fibers of the growing child. Afraid, and not
knowing of what. Unable to tell even when asked, because
she didn't know. Only at odd unexpected moments would it
be a fear of *something*. Then one night, Andy Prince told
her his eyes were bad and he had a headache. With a sigh
that broke against her shoulder he told her. But caught in
her own drama she couldn't believe in headaches. She told
him to get himself an aspirin; and that, she remembered
afterward, was the last thing she was ever to tell him.

She didn't know it then, but Andy Prince had meningitis. And after only ten days Andy Prince was dead. She
had never believed he would die. March's sarch for the
sick, the weak, and the dying would not find Andy Prince.
She'd see to that. She'd pitch her strength against the stone
an unmerciful God was bent on rolling against her mouth.
The weather too was on her side. That year it was soft,
fresh, and dry.

The air was filled with talk of Christ and lilies. And
in the chapels, unlit virgin wax candles soared against the
drapes of mourning purple. But the windows of the shops
she passed on her way to and from the Army hospital where
he was were filled with Easter. And silver- and gold-papered
eggs and fluffy grinning ghost-chickens. They grinned and
winked as she passed. Dug with their claws their little feath-
ered selves right down into the hollow darkness of her heart.
And laughed outright as she shrank from them and from
Andy Prince's screams. For five days Andy Prince screamed,
and his eyeballs walled up in a corner were stuck and blind.
Inside the room with the windows open, he lay there finally

on that high narrow white bed, his face turned from her, his fair head drawn back in a buckled way. He lay on that bed, Andy Prince did. Powerless now even to scream. He died on Easter morning. The loveliest of mornings. In the street, children passing carried colored straw baskets stuffed with the glitter of eggs bouquet'd with pink and blue and bold red ribbons. His brother the farmer came mumbling prayers from Limerick to take him back to the family grave. But even then she didn't believe he was dead, not till she saw the coffin. Then she knew. After that he came to her in dreams, Andy Prince did. He came the night his son was born dead. And for a while in Grangegorman the madhouse, till she was shifted from the open ward to the cell on her own. After that Andy Prince stopped coming.

She was in that cell for eleven long months. On a mattress on the floor. Like an animal. When she did stir she crawled on all fours. Knocked out they kept her, so that most of the time she saw nothing and heard nothing. When she did see again, the first thing she saw was frost. February frost crusting puddles in the yard like milk curdling round a babby's mouth. One morning a nurse with eyes that could shiver glass lifted her to her feet and took her out onto the landing where the windows were. There were no windows in her cell. And one morning they gave her clothes. Somebody else's. They lived a life of their own, those clothes did. She used to go where they took her.

Till a man told her she could go. But he didn't say where. "I guess he never thought he had to," Ellen Simms said, and sat remote as stone and her mouth finished was sad and quiet. Annie had been rocking slightly in her chair, tilting it back, then letting the front legs hit the floor with little taps, her hands holding the table edge for balance. She stopped rocking when Ellen Simms stopped speaking and sat now with her hands round her throat, as if unknown words were there or inside strange feelings were flowering. "I never knew," she said finally; and from the lane there was the evening sounds of women talking and kids keening. Then the metallic grush of pennies, running footsteps, and wild shouting voices.

I stirred in my chair, but round that table none of us spoke for a long time; but underneath it, Annie, patting her bare feet on the floor in an accustomed way, finally said: "But what about your house in the park and all your things in it?"

"The house and everything in it was gone," Ellen Simms said. "With the nonchalance of ownership, Andy Prince's brother let the house and everything in it go when they locked me up."

"But didn't you get anything?" I asked.

Ellen Simms shook her head. "The only thing I got out of it was the clothes I stood up in, and that crib. He sent that to the hospital. The crib instead of a prayerbook. Probably thought it would have the same desired effect."

"But could you not have gone to live with him after the hospital?" Annie asked.

"I don't know," Ellen Simms said. "All I know is I didn't. Maybe it was because I was sore," she said grimly. "Not angry sore, but hurting sore. Sore all over I was. Whether from beatings or drugs, I don't know. But my body and my mind hurt."

"So what did you do?" Annie asked, and her voice was high and ragged as she questioned, and stared at the face before her.

"Walked," Ellen Simms said. And I thought of her walking with the strides that made Annie's mother say Ellen Simms was a fella in skirts. "Away from the brother, the hospital, and where it was I had left Andy Prince. Through the soles of my shoes I walked down to what I prayed would

be the last of my several lives. On my own at first till I fell
in with others who like myself were unable to check the
drift."

"Who were they?" I asked.

Ellen Simms shook her head. "I don't know now and
I didn't care enough then to ask. Tinkers or Gipsies. One of
them, a woman, could munch glass and did, to amuse the
laundered people in the big demesnes. Another told fortunes
with a ball of hair cut from the stomach of a cat. Me!
I washed clothes and walls and floors. Doing the things I
remembered women in houses did. Then it was April again.
And another Easter. About this time of evening. We were
coming into the city and got to the bridge above, and on the
spur of the moment I decided it was time to take root. I left
them and came down this street. To this lane, to this very
house. I lay down on the stairs, thinking I would till morning. And above me some time during the night, this woman
came. Said my crying had waked her. In my sleep I was
crying, she said. She asked me if I'd come far. And I told
her, very far, hoping she'd content herself with this because
I had grown to hate the awkwardness of questions, even if
most people do settle for half answers. But she never asked
me another. Just stood over me for a long time to see in
my face the things that had happened. Then shifting herself
into great activity she told me to come in. Into this very
room. Merton, she said her name was. Pert Merton.

"I didn't then, but in the light of the morning I saw
she was old. Old and bugle-bonneted. Said she was a dealer.
The first dealer I ever knew. She asked me my name and I
gave it as Simms. My maiden name. Why I didn't give her
the other I don't know. She asked me to stay and I did. And
it was she told me how to set about dealing. What to buy
and where and how to sell. Then she went. Without a mur-

mur one night. I'd made her a cup of cocoa and was sitting
where I am now, watching her drink it. She was on that bed.
Then she said she was cold. Before Andy Prince and the
things that had happened, I might've been deterred, but I
wasn't now. So I went and lay down beside her, my arms
spread out across her, my face to her face. I prayed for God
to give her my strength. For a long time I prayed. But she
was old and tired. Mortally. And it was time, she said.
There was no reason why she should go on living. I've finished, she said. It's time. And it was and she went that day.
Left me with this room and the few poor utensils in it.
Things others hadn't valued. Like herself. It was she who
left me that cart."

"You mean the one below in the hall?" Annie asked
quickly. Ellen Simms nodded.

Annie's gaze met mine and locked till Ellen Simms
said: "Then I had to learn how to use it. A painful process
and prolonged, that was. Now I'll be glad to be rid of it."

"What'll you do now?" I asked. And beyond the windows that Ellen Simms was gazing at, the twilight was lasting and blue and still. Dragging herself up from the position
she had slumped into, she eyed me serious. "Do? Why, I'm
not so old I can't still do a good day's work. And I will for
a couple of my ladies. And I'll read. I found my way to
books late, you know. And as for money: well, I've never
been what you might call extravagant. I'll manage." She
looked at Annie. "Come next Saturday you take over where
I leave off. Providing of course your mother hasn't locked
you up in Barker's before then."

"Not if she knows what's good for her," Annie said,
but the look she threw me was swift and apprehensive.

"I truly believe you mean that," Ellen Simms said.

"I do," Annie replied. "But how come," she asked

quickly, "you never told us about Andy Prince before?"
And so started the conclusion of that conversation, the last
we were ever to have with Ellen Simms.

"Because I don't think about Andy Prince any more,"
Ellen Simms said, and her voice had changed completely.
"I couldn't, and live. Reason I told you now is to warn you
against doing what I did. Against ever becoming dependent
on anything or anybody. The way I depended on Andy
Prince. I didn't deliberately. But I did just the same, without even knowing what it was I was doing. I turned myself
into another person altogether; and was so busy doing that,
I let everything else go. All those years with my father in
that lane and all my years on the streets of this city and
everything those years had taught me. Thinking that with
Andy Prince I could afford to. Thinking I'd not need that
kind of strength again—an so when the never-expected did
happen I'd nothing to fall back on. Nothing that would take
me with sense and sensibility through the uproar. And so I
ended up in the madhouse. And why? Because with Andy
Prince and away from the lane and all I knew, I'd become
soft and useless. That's why I'm telling you now, you can't
allow yourself to be bunched or bet. What you've got to do
is hold fast to whatever it is that's taken you this far without help or benefit from clergy or state."

"But I don't know what that is," Annie said, puzzled.

"It's whatever it was made you face me when others
your age were running the other way and crying 'witch,'"
Ellen Simms said. "It's the thing that makes you brave the
shopkeepers of Dublin day after day and risk five or six
years in a reformatory every time your hand closes on a
dozen English wax candles.

"It's what made you hold Robey up to ransom last
night—and what's making you stand up to your mother and

her childish delusions of the solidity she thinks she can sur-
round herself and them useless sisters of yours with, by condemning you to that hell-hole of a factory. It's whatever it
is that makes you fight and go on fighting the way you do,"
Ellen Simms said, and, pausing, drew her hindered hand
across her mouth.

"It won't be easy going against my Ma," Annie said.

"I never thought it would be, pet," Ellen Simms said,
and her voice shattered and died; but her gaze on Annie,
who got up from the table suddenly and began to walk round
the room, was both a kindness and a darkness.

Night was coming through the windows, was filling the
corners of the room. And from the table Ellen Simms
watched it come in silence. The face of the clock on the
mantelpiece faded and then the white china dogs on either
side, and then the wall behind them.

"I should light the lamp," Ellen Simms said, returning
out of the distance. But she didn't.

"We should go," I whispered to Annie; but my voice
sounded high in the room.

"You go," she said, and continued to go round and
round us in a stiff-legged restless way.

Finally I said to Ellen Simms, "Meningitis"; and
when she didn't answer, I said: "What exactly is meningitis?" I leaned closer against the table.

"Something like pneumonia," she said, and the words
in her mouth were as smooth and as hard as marbles. With
her good hand she drew my empty plate over onto hers and
then reached out for Annie's.

"And the hospital," I asked, and because she looked at
me as if she needed reminding, I said: "They knocked you
out. How?"

"With drugs," she said. "To stop me thinking. As if

they could," she added; and slowly she began to draw everything on the table toward her. "You've seen a straitjacket?" she asked.

"They took Primmy Maggott's father away in one," I said.

"Well, on me they used drugs."

"Because you were crazy?"

"They thought I was, or pretended to," Ellen Simms said. "But I think it's only because doctors don't know yet how to cater for the desperate. They're like politicians, all slick slogans and pills."

"Why did they put you on a mattress on the floor?" I asked.

"So's I wouldn't harm myself."

"Would you have?"

"I don't know. I can't remember even nursing the intention."

"What do you remember?" I asked.

"Wanting everything to stop—the way I want Annie to stop going round and round me now," she said.

And when Annie passed her the next time round she reached out an arm and grabbed her. "You've done enough thinking and walking for one night," she said; and some remembered tenderness made her bright. Against her Annie leaned in a way she never did against her mother.

"Just stop," Ellen Simms said, and went on from there as if she had never interrupted herself. "I thought if everything did, I'd find my own way back to the person I was before Andy Prince. Only I needed time. To think and find again my own two feet. See with my own eyes instead of his. But the misguided intentions of others impeded. And not a thing stopped. Because nothing in this world is allowed to stop. Not even the sky or the streets through which the men from that hospital dragged me. They were restless. The streets. Restless the way fever is and the way this child in my arms is right now. And so were the trams. I remember the sparks of the trams made purple wounds that throbbed in the veins in the faces of the people passing. And the hands. . . ." Ellen Simms paused and her own one, slightly larger than the other and hindered and wide-knuckled, wrapped around Annie's waist, tightened, and drew close. "Hands everywhere, stretched for what they could take and grab," she said, and her eyes on me burned. "One good thing about people thinking you're mad is the way you see everything. It's like having something great and extraordinary explained. There is no deception. People stop hiding because they no longer see the need. Truth for the first time becomes lovely. You can see them being struck by the loveliness of truth. And then you hear things you never would've otherwise. For as far as they are concerned, if you're mad, you're dead anyway."

Ellen Simms paused and against her Annie settled. "I hope I never go mad," I said, after all three of us had been silent awhile.

"Being trapped is worse," Annie said.

"Being dead is worse," I said.

"No it isn't," Annie replied, "because when you're dead you don't even know you're dead."

"That's true," Ellen Simms said. "And we are all of us trapped. We are born trapped and most of us stay trapped."

"I won't," Annie said; and now herself and Ellen Simms were as close as one body. "I'm trapped now maybe, but I won't stay trapped."

"None of us would if we had any choice," Ellen Simms said. "Trouble is, we haven't. And the fact remains, we are trapped. If not by one thing, then another. If not by poverty and ignorance, then by things like drink or fear—fear of being lonely, unloved, unwanted, or of being poor or sick; or even by affection or responsibility. And sometimes the only way to free ourselves is through death or madness. Because most of the time it's more than human beings can stand."

Ellen Simms paused, and with one hand pushed back her hair; and outside in the sky the stars spread. "I don't understand why we have to," Annie said. "Stand it, I mean. What's the reason for everything? Maybe there is one, but if so I can't see it."

"If you could there would be no need to call on God as often as we do," Ellen Simms said.

"I don't call on him," Annie replied swiftly. "I've never asked him for as much as a glass of water in my life. All I want to know is why things are the way they are, and I don't care who answers just so long as somebody does."

"Nobody will, because nobody can," Ellen Simms said. "We know just so much and no more."

"Well, it's not nearly enough," Annie said. She drew herself out of Ellen Simms' clasp. "I bet somebody knows."

"Well, whoever it is, is keeping it to themselves, pet," Ellen Simms said, and stirred in her chair to ease her back and stand up. She was dark and upright in her man's striped shirt and blue cotton apron.

"I must light the lamp," she said, but for a moment longer she stood there, her right hand on Annie's shoulder. The sounds coming in at us now from the house and the lane were night sounds. Sounds of kids being called, doors and windows closing, the lamplighter's bike and bell; and as Ellen Simms moved against the glass of her windows the gaslight from the lane was sharp and sudden.

"I'll find out," Annie said. "One of these days I'll know the reason for everything." We stood on either side of the table, and to the double-wicked lamp hanging on the wall

over the mantelpiece Ellen Simms put a match. There was
a smoky flare through which Annie and I blinked at each
other as if we were strangers or ghosts. Then the light was
caught and coffined by the glass globe Ellen Simms lowered
over it.

"I never did say what I came to say," Annie said.

"You can again," Ellen Simms said. "There'll be other
nights." She spoke stiffly, her back to the lamp, her face in
shadow. "And I'll see the pair of you on Saturday."

"Yes," Annie said, and began to unstick the hair that
all evening had lain on her forehead.

"Come on," I said, and together we moved through the
lamplight to the door. We looked back from it.

"Will you be all right?" Annie's eyes, rising to the
square dark face coming across the room toward us, were
soft and thoughtful.

"Of course," said Ellen Simms. She touched Annie's
face with her hindered hand. And before the door closed
on us she touched mine.

"It felt like stone," I said when we reached the hall.
"What did?" Annie asked, but her mind was elsewhere.

"Ellen Simms' hand," I said; and in the hall under the
stairs, Annie stood beside the cart scrubbed and empty. Her
hands closed on the rounded handle.

"The week will be endless," she said. She let go the
handle. "Will we ever get through it?" she asked; and, in
the lane, we stopped to look up at Ellen Simms' windows.
But only the lamplight filtering through the lace drawn curtains showed.

ℰ10

Under a leering blue sky two things happened the following day. At fifteen Paddy Paddy, big-fisted, rowdy, and cruel, had found the world too ruthless even for him; and, tying a sack over his head as he had done and seen done with needless cats and dogs, had let himself down into the slow water of the canal. And with Barker's biscuit factory shadowing her like some creature of nightmares black and terrifying and many-armed, Annie entered upon a new time of waiting. Feeling trapped and with no real prospect of getting the few pounds she would need to begin dealing, she tore through the early part of Monday morning's bens with a restlessness and an agitation that was painful. And on Fitzwilliam Square, to the remarks joking or otherwise of the cinder-pickers, she could make no reply that fitted, although with Biddser Mulvey and Mollow Ross she tried.

For a while, like a singer who has to sing a song she doesn't know, she tried to catch the air of the square and follow; but after a time she gave up trying to mingle the things of yesterday with the things of today, and soon she broke down into a state that was silent and wooden. Once with his rapid breath flooding over her face, she crossed swords with Scraps, but her heart wasn't in it; and once with a hollow sorriness for Paddy Paddy thickening her voice, she said: "I wonder why he did it," and once she shouted in angry loudness when a gowger we didn't know, acting flash and soiled with some sensuality, jazzily crossed her path.

Around about eight on our way up from one basement and down into another, seeing Maggie Hyland with a group of cronies prance into the square from the direction of Baggot Street, she said, "Oh," and stood motionless, and then suddenly burst out laughing when Hyland and her gang, catching sight of us, braked and with a smart about-turn took to their heels. "I don't know when I've seen anything as funny," she said, and behind us Jim Mac and his sister Carmel stopped and craned their necks to see.

"What's funny?" Carmel Mac asked, but Annie just looked at the sullen face and the two poor plaits framing it and didn't answer.

"I'm selling me cinders," Jim Mac said, shifting his weight from foot to foot and trying to still his timid shaking. He looked at Annie. "I have to," he said, and we were about to ask why and he was on the verge of telling us why when Carmel nudged him roughly to silence.

"The whole square doesn't have to know our business," she told him, while I asked what he was wanting for his cinders and watched him drop his sack to the ground.

"I don't know," he said, "but they're all good."

"So who's buying them?" Annie asked, making no attempt to stifle the impatience she always felt in Carmel Mac's presence. But her face I noticed was suddenly brighter and her voice certainly a whole lot lighter than it had been.

"He thought you might," Carmel Mac sneered. "And a sadder piece of foolishness I've never heard. Because where in this wide world would you get that class of money on a Monday morning?"

Calmly Annie eyed her. "If you think you're going to stand there hindering my passage and sniffling remarks I don't want to hear, you've another think coming," she said.

Carmel Mac's glance fell. "Well," she said and shrugged. "It just about makes my stomach turn, listening to people who don't have any sense."

"Your stomach is easily turned," Annie said, "but you're not, I hope, referring to me by any chance," and in her sharp glance and on the curve of her lips there was a wryness and the bare suggestion of a challenging smile.

Carmel Mac backed down. "*If you must know*, I was referring to my thick of a brother," she said. "For just imagine anyone in their right senses asking you to buy a sack of cinders or a sack of anything else for that matter."

"Is that so? Well, I might surprise you, wise-mouth," Annie said, and turning her attention to Jim Mac, asked: "How much you wanting for them cinders?"

"He was thinking in terms of shillings," Carmel Mac answered before Jim could.

"Well, thinking costs nothing!" Annie, easing the sack on her back, made as if to walk away.

"What do *you* think they're worth?" Jim Mac asked quickly, and himself and Annie looked at each other.

"Sevenpence," Annie said. Jim glanced at his sister, but all she did was sigh and shrug grudgingly. He turned to Annie.

"Done," he said.

"Only naturally, before I buy, I got to see the kind of cinders you and bright-eyes have selected," Annie said.

"Fair enough," Jim Mac replied. And on the ground opened the mouth of his sack wide. Looking hard at the contents Annie raked with her free hand through the cinders and then nodded her satisfaction.

"I've an idea," she said, and her glance, at once speculative and gleaming, met mine. "But first how much money you got?" she asked.

"Thruppence," I said.

"And I've fourpence," she said. "Now if you and me was to put that together we could buy—and why we should is something I'll tell you after." Reluctantly I parted with my thruppence and Annie handed over her fourpence; then pointedly waiting until the MacDonalds were gone and well out of hearing, she said: "You and me is in business."

Seeing her looking for some sign of appreciation or approval, I asked "How?" and heard her say "Simple," and saw a warm glow creep up under her skin and flood her cheeks.

"We get a shilling for that sack of cinders, right!"

"Maybe," I said; and in the fashion of the follower the shrug I gave was meant to express my across-the-board pessimism and was done now as always on principle, at whatever was suggested before I went along with it.

"No 'maybe' about it," she replied smartly. "Why," she said, and her voice rose in wonder, "there isn't a woman the length and breadth of Rock Street who wouldn't pay a shilling for that sack of cinders there. And at a shilling a sack, that means fivepence profit, doesn't it?" I nodded. "So supposing, with the shilling we make on that, we buy another sack at sevenpence—that would mean tenpence clear profit, wouldn't it?"

"But who else would sell at Jim Mac's price?" I asked.

"There isn't a soul walking these pavements this morning who wouldn't," she said, and her glance roped in the square and the people on it.

"Even if they did, we haven't the money to buy," I said.

"But if we sell what we have right now, we could this afternoon," Annie said. "And I've another idea," she added. "Just supposing," she began slowly, "we get a corner in Mr. Cullen's stable yard and make whoever sells bring the cinders to us there. . . . That way we don't have to lug them from here ourselves. Also we could store up in the yard and from there you could get the cinders to the customers quicker."

"And what would you be doing?" I asked when she paused.

"Me! Why I'll stay behind, keep shop and do the buying. I'm better at buying than you are."

"But we don't have a shop," I said.

"True," she replied. "But what's to prevent us making some class of shelter ourselves? Nothing that I can see. And it would look better. But we'll deal with that when we come to it. The important thing right this minute is to get word out that from now till Saturday you and me is in business—buying!"

And there and then word went out. Putting on the man's tweed cap from which the peak had been ripped, Annie made the announcement herself. Briskly and from the top of the steps we were standing at, and with no trace now of the weight that had all morning thickened her voice, she began bawling: "Fire!" at the top of her lungs, stopping only when she was sure she had the square's attention, and only when the pickers who came at the double or at a steady respectable trot had gathered.

To those head-straining to see the fire, and to others with breath coming in pants of heavy complaint at finding none, she said, "Ah, push off"; and at others booing she made flashing angry darts from which they made quick retreat. Demanding order from the crowd that remained, and Biddser Mulvey and Brennan the Builder were among them and so was Aggie the Saint, she unfolded to them her plans and, pausing finally, concluded with: "On one condition," and pausing again, and this time dramatically, said: "The cinders must be delivered to *me,* in Mr. Cullen's stable yard in Rock Street. I'm paying sevenpence a sack," she told the astonished assembly, looking pleased with herself until menacing shouts and protests of "Arse nesting," and "Ripe robbery," forced her to gradually up the price to ninepence, thereby cutting the profit she had hoped to make down to almost half.

But even so, with no overheads to meet, we were still onto a good thing, I thought, as I watched her face and shout down a burly scrawny-headed man who came mooching through the crowd and up the steps toward her, his thick red-lipped mouth rolling out sonorous charges of "Capitalist" and indistinct syllables of pink-tinged wisdom until Brennan the Builder, reaching out a long and powerful arm, dragged him back into the crowd and Annie went on to say that she would also buy clean bits of colored silk of the kind that would make Agganastays. But the price for these, she told Aggie the Saint who asked, depended on the amount offered and upon the quality and condition of the silk.

These were for sale to the nuns in certain convents, she explained later that afternoon, after we had sold with no trouble the cinders we had, and while we were putting up a lean-to in a corner of Mr. Cullen's yard. With black housebacks crowding round us, we built the lean-to with iron bedheads of differing sizes and made the roof out of a piece of

corrugated iron resting across them. Because Annie wanted
it to look like a shop, across the front we placed a plank on
two empty oil drums, and on the wall under the roof she
hung a sad old stained circus poster to take the bare look
off it. She didn't need a pencil or a notebook but, she said
seriously, she thought she should have both, and leaving me
behind went up to Mr. Doyle's shop and swiped them. She
came back with the notebook in her hand and a red pencil
stuck behind her right ear, and then went behind the counter
to wait for our first customer.

Three youngwans came first. Sent, Annie suspected, by
Maggie Hyland, and not to sell but to look. Walking slow
in clean dresses, two of them had satin ribbons in their hair,
and they came with assumed carelessness right up and passed
us and the lean-to in single file. In the old days of that summer, Annie would've taken them on, or asked them what
they wanted and what they were gawking at; and then at the
very last, when it was plain why they had come, and she had
felt the cold blast of their triumph, she would have sent them
running in windy panic with an angry shout. But now all she
did was watch them quietly and without anger, outstaring
them stare by stare till on a mocking laugh, all three went
running from the yard, just as the first of the cinder-pickers,
heavy in clumsy boots, tore into it.

A lean gray-haired angry-faced woman, dragged off
balance by the child she carried in one arm and the sack on
her back she was holding onto with the other, yelled, "Which
of youse chiselers is buying?" and stood peering expectantly
from me to Annie.

"What d'yah mean, chiselers!" Annie flared. "That's
no civilized way to come selling," she said.

"At ninepence a sack, who in the name of Jasus is selling?" the woman asked. "It's condoning sinful pastimes I

am, God help me," she said, and dropped her sack to the ground.

"You don't have to," Annie said, watching her closely. "After all, nobody sent for you."

"In my unfortunate circumstances, nobody had to," the woman growled, and shuffled forward, dragging the sack behind her.

She dumped it at my feet and stretched her hand out to Annie. "Well, c'mon," she cried impatiently, but Annie wasn't going to be rushed, not into anything.

"Hold your horses," she said, "we have to see what you're selling first."

The woman, checked, stared at her. "Well, be Jasus," she sneered, "but I remember you when you were nothing more than a frisky spring running bollix-naked through the squares, but overnight you seem to have developed into a sensible summer." She turned to me. "An as for you, day-dreaming there—it would suit you better to be making yourself useful." And I did, and quickly, while she watched me run my hand through the cinders in her sack, and finding neither stones nor clinkers I nodded to Annie. She began to count penny after penny into the woman's open hand, until the woman, looking her straight in the face said, "An it's a favor I doing youse"; and right away Annie stopped counting.

"Nope. No favors," she said. "I don't want no favors from you or anyone else. Every time someone does me a favor I end up losing the Goddamn shift off my back."

"But look at the price you're——" the woman began, but Annie cut right through her.

"Missus," she said, "take yourself and your cinders elsewhere, because my favor days is all over. Can't afford them."

"Ah, for Christ's sake keep your hair on," the woman cried, and shifted the child in her arms.

"All right then," Annie said, "but understand you're doing us no favors and I don't want no bickering from you either, mind, because you don't have to sell to us—nobody's forcing you to."

"Maybe they shagging well ought to," the woman said, and into her stretched hand Annie continued to count the money.

I emptied the cinders she had brought into a sack of our own, then gave the woman hers. She grabbed it and, with a bitter curse ringing in our ears and muttering vigorously, turned away and at the gateway of the yard pushed her way past the first of the pickers coming through it. Drunk or just high-spirited I didn't know, and with the three shillings we had started out with now reduced to two and thruppence, I couldn't wait to find out. I'd have to sell what cinders we had before we could buy more; so leaving Annie, with her eyes narrowed suspiciously, to handle the newcomers, I plundered off to do the selling.

We operated this way through what was left of Monday, right through Thursday morning when, as if at some prearranged signal, every cinder-picker off the squares made their way into the stable yard precisely at the same time. Urgently intent on the task we had set ourselves, there was no time to find out why, or pause to wonder at voices no longer nagging heaven, or decipher thoughts in eyes that peered and pierced; no time either to examine the sacks they brought, and I didn't, and neither did Annie. Instead, without even touching the ground, a sack hoisted high on the top of a back was lifted over onto mine, and before a penny had changed hands I was on my way out the yard to the street and what I imagined was another satisfied customer.

And this way time swung from one minute to another until the sun, imbedded like a brass nailhead on the lid of a coffin all that day, dulled and faded, and finally gave way to exhaustion and the gentle lavender dusk of evening.

It was about eight o'clock and Annie and I were sitting on the ground outside the lean-to, and behind us on the plank, resting on the oil drums, our sacks all nicely folded and smoothed out ready for the next day, when the low humming boo started. It silenced the distant noise of the traffic on Rock Street and, gradually growing louder, swallowed up Annie's voice counting for the tenth time the six pounds we had made, and, getting deeper, drowned out the noise of the tin box she was putting the money into; and shaping itself into a menacing roar of anger flooded down the lane and broke like a tidal wave through the gateway of Mr. Cullen's stable yard. Jumping to our feet I remembered a march; a silent ominous march Annie and I had seen one night in O'Connell Street. A very silent scraggly march of the unemployed—with nobody saying anything—just people, a mass of people, flowing down the street toward the Piller; and then from the theem of thought I came and moved and stood close to Annie to face the chanting challenge of the people surging across the yard toward us.

I saw a woman I knew, but not well, yelling savagely, and another behind her belting forward with a basin full of bricks, and ducked from a shower of them flung not from her but from some other hating hand in the crowd. I heard Annie say, "It's the cinders," and a thought shaped itself up in my head. I remembered the unaccountable gaiety of the cinder-pickers that morning in the yard, just as bright-eyed Sally Early facing Annie screamed: "It's the stones, you mean!" and flung a bucket of them on the ground at our feet. "A whole shagging shilling's worth of stones that young gurrier there sold me," she roared and drew aside to let her husband who had come with her, step up and take over.

I saw his jaws work and knew his mind was pulsing noisy doubt, and through the midst of the tumult I saw wedged in the crowd Maggie Hyland and two of the beggars, and thought she shouted something about Ellen Simms before she was pressed back as hands, hundreds of hands, tore at me and Annie and at the lean-to behind us. I saw a man coatless and shirtless, tug and tug at the roof of the lean-to, till it collapsed under his weight and the weight of the kids struggling with him and with each other to be the first to tear what was left of it to pieces.

And then Annie sprang, and from her clouded fury those nearest us shrank back while her eyes, glittering with fight, swept over them. "Back!" she roared. "Back, every Goddamn wan of youse!"

"And back I want every shagging penny of that shilling that youngfella made me in foolishness part with," Sally Early screamed.

"And that's not all you'll get if you don't take your dirty idle hands off us," Annie shouted, and my eyes lit on a lone woman standing midway between the crowd and the gate, making frantic signals to us. Knowing somehow that a purpose different from the one that had brought the others to the yard had guided her into it, I wanted to know the reason; but with the crowd tightening round us there was no way of finding out.

"I want that shilling back," Sally Early's husband snarled, his mouth slavering a rage he hadn't the guts to loose.

"And me mine," a woman I remembered buying from me shrilled; and now round us voices everywhere were rising and chanting cantankerous demands. Stiffened under the

weight of the woman's hands on my shoulders, I heard
Annie tell her she'd better remove them, and she did, with
a yelp from the swipe Annie gave her; and then telling them
she'd give none of them nothing if they laid hands on us
again. The chanting stopped.

"Who among this pack bought from you," Annie
asked, and turning, watched to see where my glance fell.

"Mrs. Early did," I said, "and her," I pointed. "And
her," I said and pointed again, and Annie opened the tin
box clutched to her chest and began to hand out shilling
after shilling until the murmuring stopped, and snarls and
heaped abuse on us and on the generations that bore us was
coming at us from a safe distance; and as one after another
of them streeled back across the yard and the only things
left in it was ourselves and the ruins of the lean-to, and the
woman who had not come with the crowd: "Them cinder-
pickers are a low filty lot," Annie said, and against the wall
where the lean-to had been she flung the empty tin box hard.
"I'll never forgive them for playing that lousy scurvy trick,"
she said. "They deliberately filled them sacks with stones
and that's why they all came here together this morning—
knowing if they did we'd not have time to look proper at
what they were offering. Apart from the fact that they have
beggared us they were very nearly having us murdered."
She paused and, looking from where it was the tin box had
landed, stared with troubled eyes into the eyes of the woman
coming toward us.

"I didn't think youse would've come out of that alive,"
the woman said.

"We nearly didn't," Annie replied. "And it would've
been just as well if we hadn't because they left us with
nothing."

The woman didn't try to console, knowing she couldn't.
Instead: "You're Annie Murphy, aren't you?" she asked.

"Why?" Annie, uncertain now, questioned cautiously.

"Because if you are I've news for you," she replied. "And it can't be broidered," she added. "It's about Ellen Simms," she said and paused.

"What about her?" Annie asked.

"Nothing, except she was knocked down," the woman said, "kicked to a pulp she was, be a horse and dray. Wan a Guinnesses. This morning in Dame Street. She's in the hospital. Below in St. Vincent's. I believe they had to scoop up off the cobbles what was left of her."

"I don't believe you," Annie said flatly.

"You don't have to," the woman replied, and her coat, the remnant of a piece of Genoa silk, sighed like the sallow skin of her face into depressed dips. For a minute the sound she was making was like those dry sounds of high summer or like the whispering feet of mice on bare boards. "Only I knew youse were great with her so I thought I'd tell you," she said.

She backed from us thoughtful, and turning, walked slow across the yard to the gate. I looked at Annie. She stood stiff from this new blow. Half turning her face from me I heard her breath sob, and I knew it wasn't from hurt— not yet, but from the mind's intuition.

"C'mon," I said; and as we went across the yard I felt sick and, as we reached the top of the lane, afraid. At the top of the lane we turned left, and at the top of Rock Street left again for the canal, and the canal-side road that led down to St. Vincent's.

Square and marble the entrance hall of St. Vincent's was. It smelled of homemade beeswax and ether and soap. It gaped silence, the high wide hall, the serpent twist of

stairs going up from it. Brown polished stairs on which nuns
let themselves down quietly. The silence hung in long stern
folds and it couldn't be disturbed. Ever. Christ on a cross
stared at us with the jowled faces of dead Reverend Mothers, and He and them were frightening. There was no
trespassing beyond certain set boundaries, the doorman said.
He came out of a little room off the hall on our right and
stood before us. He wore a brown smock, and looked down
at Annie's bare feet and then at her shorn head. A full-
bellied, clean-skinned, smug-faced bastard of a man. Tall
and snakeheaded with poor hair plastered with oil tight to
the scalp and razored to a short back and sides. We knew
him by sight and had hated him for years, and he us. And
now a fight with him for admission was helping to puncture
misery.

"This isn't a doss-house, you know," he said.

"Well, you could've fooled me," Annie told him.

"Only gain admission here at certain hours and on certain days," he said, ignoring Annie. "And them days and
hours is——" he began, but Annie cut through him.

"We know what them days and hours is," she said,
"and we also know a million ways of getting into this place.
So make up your mind and quick, because either we go
through here or we go through one of the others."

"If you can find them," Snakehead said, and pushed us
out through the door.

"We'll find them," Annie said from the steps. And we
did. Down the lane behind the hospital to a passage behind
the dead house we went. And from there to a door that led
to stairs endless, that led to landings where flowers had been
put for the night, to wards long with clearings down the
middle and on each side white-quilted ghost beds. Between
them white-painted lockers stood, some holding tumblers or

white enamel basins, and at both ends of every ward, blue and red lamps smouldered at the feet of statues of the Virgin.

From the men's wards we went into the women's, moving quietly from bed to bed—straying through a nighttime wilderness of parquet floors and pain-riddled folds of lonely silences, looking into faces that sometimes drew back from what might be expected of them, or at a tear jerking itself stubborn from under lids, and which Annie even in her hurry paused to wipe away. Sometimes on our journey from one ward to another we had to hide in doorways from the solid swirl of a skirt swishing round the black-stockinged leg of a nurse or from the murmuring voices of nuns on their way to or from somewhere.

And then we found her. We found Ellen Simms. Tumbled across her in a ward in a corner under a ceiling propped with giant painted beams. Cautiously eyeing the black eyes narrowed to a gleam, we approached her, and beside her stood in a silence that, after the first shocking intake of breath, stabbed like needles.

"It's us, Ellen," Annie said, "it's only us," and, raising the corners of the top sheet, she touched lightly the broken mouth and what looked like a trickle of saliva or maybe milk that she had tried to drink in deference to obedience. "Do you know us, Ellen," Annie's eyes and voice stroked the face that had been beaten savage and the wide mobile mouth that distorted to make sounds. "We heard and we came, so's you wouldn't be afraid, we came, and we'll stay," Annie said; and, close to Ellen Simms now, we could see plain the yellow and black lacerations under a mauvish smudge that covered the whole face; and suddenly, as if to prevent us seeing this or more, Ellen Simms turned her face sideways.

Toward the black mass of hair thick-bunched and matted, Ellen Simms turned; and when Annie fisted it, it lay thick and heavy and damp on her hand. "Do you want anything?" Annie asked; but Ellen Simms could make no reply, and for a minute I thought I heard Annie's lips issue hers— or maybe it was Ellen Simms' mind's gnaw in sudden and violent prayer.

And then a voice, a somber voice behind us, was saying sharply: "And what, may I ask, are you doing here?" and above us two nuns stood. The tallest of them unwound from a great height and put her hand on Annie's shoulder; but Annie roughly shook it off, and I allowed myself instead to be drawn from the bed. "How did you children get in here?" the tall nun asked, while the other, who I guessed was a novice, stood with her hands in her sleeves at the foot of the bed and let her eyes skim its length before they came to rest at last on Annie and then on the bed's torn and battered burden.

"I asked you a question," the tall nun said impatiently, and I answered it: "We came in through the dead house," I said.

"Well, you won't have to go out through the dead house. But you must come away now," she said; and in the dusk, straddling us, she firmly grabbed Annie and then me, and drew us with her down the full length of the ward and out onto the landing that had been darkened for the night. "What are you doing here?" she asked, and left the little nun to close the door of the ward behind us.

"We came to see Ellen Simms," I said, because Annie didn't look as if *she* could, and my eyes traveling up over the fold marks in the nun's scapular met the gaze she was letting fall squarely on me.

"And who *are* you," she asked.

"We live beside her," Annie said. "And we want to know what happened," she added.

"At this hour of the night," the nun sounded surprised.

"At any hour of the night," Annie said, and the nun and herself took each other's measure.

"I'm afraid there's nothing to tell," the nun said, while Annie's gaze searched her face slowly. "Except that there was an accident. A horse and dray. I believe she fell under it."

"Under the dray?" Annie asked.

The nun shook her head. "No, under the feet of the horse."

Annie stared up at the nun while I saw the horse. It was closer to me than the nun was. And it was black and shiny and it stood against a wall that had been whitewashed. It stood on trembling legs and shook all over in apprehension. And fear streamed. Streamed in folds as thick as wax. I saw Ellen Simms. Saw her tall and bent, the features seasoned and warm and twisted in sudden fright. And then I saw the raised front hooves. I saw ropes of hair torn from neat, coiled braids; then between Ellen Simms and me the nun standing over us spread Ellen Simms' muck-spattered shawl.

"Is Ellen Simms very bad?" Annie asked, and her face now was bared and intense but wiped clean as a slate of all expression.

"She is dangerously ill," the nun—who must have been new to the hospital because she had not yet become inhuman —replied, and her dry white lips moved sure over her words. "But," she said, "you must run off home now, for this is no time of the night to be running the streets."

"Will Ellen Simms die?" Annie asked. And she repeated the question before the nun, making a washing movement with her hands, said, "The patient is dangerously ill." Against her thighs Annie's hands opened and spread flat. The nun looked into her face, but what it concealed could only be guessed at.

"Her relatives have been notified," the nun said, although we hadn't asked.

"She has none," Annie said.

"I believe she has some in Limerick," the nun replied. And I remembered Ellen Simms telling us about Andy Prince's brother. I was about to remind Annie but the nun prevented me. "But here," she said, "hurry off home now, and you may make inquiries again tomorrow."

"What happened to Ellen Simms' cart?" I asked. The nun stared blankly.

"She was pushing one," I said quickly.

"If she was there can't be anything left of it," the nun said. And she moved, and as she did the imported serge of habit moaned and rustled. She shooed us down the dark corridor to the head of the stairs and then came down them with us.

"We're coming back in the morning," Annie said, and her voice and her stance implied she would brook no interference with intentions. "Will you tell Ellen Simms?" she asked.

The nun, encountering the raised eyes, nodded but said nothing; and across the marble floor of the hall Snakehead came, and chewing the green bile of impotence, stared grim. He drew back a heavy bolt, swung open the door, and without a thank-you we passed out onto the steps.

Across the road from us the trees in the Green were heavy and dark. For a second their ordinariness stunted and confused. In and out of them sparrows and pigeons swooped and pecked with remorseless industry. I glanced at Annie, but her too-direct gaze was focused on the Green.

"The cart is gone," I said suddenly. "Smashed to smithereens," I said, and waited and waited for her to break the silence that was like a knife in my side. But she didn't. "Things happen," I said. Things happened, I remembered

Ellen Simms saying. Things you had to accept. The world is
big and mysterious, she said. It can't be grasped at once.
Understanding is a painful process and comes slowly with
knowledge, like reading and writing. Everything can't be
explained.

"I wish I was old," Annie often said. "I wish I was
old because then I'd know things. When a person's old they
know everything." But now standing on the steps of the
hospital, she said nothing, only looked until her eyes grew
dim with looking, and then she went down the steps that
she was to bully and fight her way up and down three times
a day for the next two—until Saturday evening when what
she called "the waiting time" ended altogether.

Loaded with stuff looted from certain shops in Rock
Street we had come. Stuff for Ellen Simms. Oranges and
apples—biscuits covered with pink cream and a whole pound
of the tobacco Ellen Simms liked. And in a room off the
square marble hall where we had been put to wait by Snakehead on orders from the nun, we sat. And waited. A big
airy room it was, lined from floor to ceiling with books and
sparsely furnished with a desk, a prie-dieu, a horsehair
black sofa and a grouping of chairs round an oval-shaped
table. With our backs to the window splintered with city
sounds, we sat facing each other across the table, listening
to the hall outside, to footsteps and voices that sought advice, directions that hung on the ethered air for a second,
then went away. Up over our heads in her bed in the corner
of the ward, Ellen Simms lay dying. We knew she was
dying. Snakehead told us the minute we set foot in the hall,
and again a fat slovenly nun with a stovey breath who was
all on then for getting rid of us till Annie, pushing past her
and heading for the stairs, had crashed headlong into the
nun we knew, coming down.

The nun, looking down the distance that separated,

stopped abruptly, and Annie, staring up at her, stood crouched and hulked and said: "Ellen Simms is dying, isn't she?" She looked over Annie to Snakehead and the nun who, with him, had come running to prevent us reaching the ward and Ellen Simms, and her glance dismissed him.

"We want to see her," Annie said, but the nun shook her head.

"It's not possible," she said. "Not now."

"But we have to," Annie pleaded. "We know her," she said. "We know her and she knows us. We have to see her."

"It wouldn't do you or her any good if you could." The nun glanced at me.

"But she shouldn't die on her own," Annie cried, and her arms closed round the stuff she carried. "Ellen Simms will think we've forgotten. . . ."

"Right now, child, Ellen Simms has forgotten she was ever born," the nun said. "And soon even for you, Ellen Simms will survive only in . . ."

"Please, Sister," Annie's voice could be heard now over the wilder disorder of trolleys rattling, the thud of a door closing, and the quickened murmurings of human intercourse. "I won't cause any trouble or anything," she said. "I just want her to know . . ." Annie paused and her gaze, frantic, went past the nun on the stairs to the Gothic arch of stone on the landing above her and beyond that the flight of stairs that led to the ward where Ellen Simms was.

And guessing Annie's intentions, the nun, with a worried frown, reached out, and her hand closed on Annie's locked arms. "Come," she said. "Come with me." And Annie, powerless now to do other than she was told, went with her, back down to the hall and to the room the nun told Snakehead to show us into. "You may wait here," the nun said, "but only if you promise not to try and reach the ward or Ellen Simms."

With every sense now stretched at a painful attention, Annie stood and said nothing; then lifting her head she stared straight up at the nun and said: "Yes, I promise. But oh Jesus, it's not right!" she cried, as if protesting, not at the nun, but at some terrible contraction of her heart; and at a signal from the nun, Snakehead closed the door on us.

We waited without talking, Annie's eyes hidden from me by the fall of lashes, until the door opened, and we knew, seeing the nun standing there, what had happened. For unlike Peter, the nun's very thoughts betrayed her. In the room she stood over us, saying nothing till a bell rang out somewhere; then all she said was, "Ellen Simms is dead," and her voice lasted into the bell. It was time for Saturday's Compline, and in anticipation of the event the night and the nun closed in. "Come into the chapel and say a prayer for the repose of the soul of Ellen Simms," she said. And we did, following her into what had once been a concert hall until made obsolete by the endowment of a grateful mayor-elect whose portrait hung in the room we had waited in. In a pew where the nun had put us, opposite the choir, we knelt, but not with heads lowered. On a wall on our right I saw Christ was where they had nailed him. He had a blue face and bronze eyelids. Underneath the lids he was a man with sad eyes.

It was cold in the chapel, and with only ourselves on one side and the nuns on the other the space was enormous. As the nuns intoned the first psalm, I saw the eyes of the one we knew make a firm line across the dreary chasm of plain chant to us in our pew. From long habit I stirred myself, but Annie, who had never learnt much about the chapel or its ways, stayed as she was. But then Annie's father and mother didn't believe there was a limit to time. Did Ellen Simms, I wondered. She certainly hadn't expected to die. Even though common sense should have prepared her for its eventuality. She was a reasonable woman and reason alone would have told her your death sentence is written into your palm the day you're born. They would be moving her from the bed above now to a cold slab in the dead house. Or her brother-in-law would be taking her down to Limerick. He would bury her alongside Andy Prince. Because . . .

"Gloria Patri, et Filio, et Spiritu Sancto"

. . . because that's where Ellen Simms would want to be. From my blank gaze I saw a nun in the choir turn. There would be no cart for Annie now. Annie wouldn't be a dealer. And all that had happened up to this very night would be put away. Annie's mother had won, just as she knew she would. And now they would be put away—the efforts. The plans. Put away and, without anyone being the wiser, mulled over or maybe left altogether . . .

"Completi sunt dies Mariae, ut paretet Filium
sun primogenitum."

"I walked down to what I hoped would be the last of my several lives." The extinct voice mingled. The voices of ghosts could melt bones. Across from us the nuns rose to their feet and the two saucered lights on the floor each side of the altar rose and bent but didn't go out.

"In manus tuas, Domine, commendo spiritum meum."

And now the chanter and the choir were speaking alternately. I heard them and beside me the sounds Annie was making. It was a keen. A low keen of grief myself and the nuns heard. I saw a few of them glance sly and knew they were wanting Annie to stop—wanting the voice to die; but she didn't stop, not even to please the nuns, because what she felt now would tolerate no separation.

Annie was crying for Ellen Simms and a man who died at Easter. A man named Andy Prince. Annie cried real tears. Crying for a hindered hand, a blue cotton apron, and a clay pipe. And her crying, at first just a terrible throb, burst loose suddenly and on the first line of the Te Lucis, trumpeted its own laceration across the very dome of the chapel. It couldn't be listened to; but it was, because there was no armor against the rain of sounds. It tore itself with the brutal authority of sorrow, right across the voices of the choir, who faltered indecisively, then ticked a minute like a clock, prim and slow, before they gave way altogether. And like me they listened, the nuns did, to Annie frankly and openly, as her crying fought and struggled with itself under the chapel's roof and, scalpel-sharp, found incisions where before none had existed.

"Per Jesus Christum Dominum."

Under the starched shadow of her coif, some nun's throat muscles strained. There was a sudden shocking moment of awareness when I saw the staring nuns, and then a smothering flash of panic as across the distance I saw the nun whose face we knew swim. In the smouldering light of the chapel there was a crumbling, a scattering, as of ashes in an earthquake, and from it I had an impression of Annie dragging herself, rising defiant, her mouth filled with protest that before she hadn't made, but which could be heard between the crying that came now from the very depths of her body. I felt them come at me through the red of her pinny, could almost touch the fight going on. The fight which had so often threatened her with destruction, and her crying now echoed the long barely subjugated cry of the lonely, the unwanted, the lovely who are not loved, whose expressions are of sleep, solitariness, savaged under the hobnailed boots of the selfish, the uncaring, the untouched, the discreetly averted eyes and piously folded hands of the world through which they make their apologetic way.

It was against humanity's and God's indifference that Annie cried, for the pity He had not shown Ellen Simms or her, for the love she had never had, and for Ellen Simms' lonely death—for the cart, she cried, and for hours round a table in a room in a lane. And when she stopped crying her body vibrated with all she had, during the length of the Te Lucis, experienced, and as the nuns began the Canticle of Simeon, with her eyes closing in tiredness, she struggled up out of the pew to go. Surprised them nuns musta been when they touched their chests, not to find their hearts broken, I thought, as I followed her out onto the narrow aisle down which she clattered noisy, dropping oranges, apples, biscuits, and tobacco as she went; and to which I paid no mind because over her now silence hung, and sleep and loss and sorrow brooded.

11

In the morning in the sun, Rock Street was idle and lonesome with Sunday. Up it, boneless gulls swooped over Saturday's garbage filling the gutters; and crawthumpers clutching prayerbooks took the somber path to the first Mass of the day. From Miz Robey's house a lone man came, and as he passed, turned to look at me as if I owed him something. For a minute I thought of asking, but the night before had taken heavy toll of my spirits so I let it pass. Remembering then a terrible dream I had had, I crossed the street to avoid recalling the details and, shading my eyes against the light, looked through the glass of Mr. Doyle's shop window to check the time. The clock showed just on seven, and at seven on the dot there was a shout, and in the Sunday emptiness I could, as she hurried up the lane, hear the balls of Annie's heels hitting the cobbles.

At first sight of me the smile on her face spread into a laugh as we came together in the middle of the street, and as she handed me a cut of bread buttered she said, "You never called for me."

"I know."

"Why not?" she asked. Because I didn't want to rush into the emptiness that I know is waiting for me, I said; but only to myself. I shrugged instead.

"Who woke you?" I asked.

"Mollser," Annie grinned. "Guess what she was going on about?" she asked.

"Money," I said.

She nodded. "Money and disease. Says money and disease are great levelers." Her grin was now malicious. "There's no mistake about it but Mollser always comes from the lusty drifts of sleep with great discoveries. . . . Is that nice?" she asked, and she meant the bread and I nodded.

"What'll we do today?" she asked. She looked up at the sky. "I thought maybe we'd go to Sandymount," she said.

I stared surprised. "But last night you said we couldn't go anywhere today, that you'd have to use it getting ready for tomorrow."

"I know I did. But I washed my head last night, so we'd have today. It just might be our last," she said; and from a chapel somewhere, bells groped at the unexplored morning.

"I wouldn't bet on it," I said. "For instance," I asked, "what happens if you're not taken on in Barker's tomorrow?"

"I will be," she said. She eyed me straight. "I've got to be," she said, and her manner now was the thoroughgoing one she used when she made pronouncements. "Besides, why wouldn't I be?"

"Because," I said, "you're only twelve and you're supposed to be fourteen for work in a factory—that's the law."

"The law! You try telling Mollser about the law. And

law or no law, by the time Mollser's through with me I'll look an awful lot more than twelve. They are going to do me up," she said, and the thought made her restless because she began to swing back her arms and clap the palms of her hands together. "I heard them talking last night," she said. "Mollser and Alice. They thought I was asleep but I wasn't. I was thinking about all them wrecked plans and I heard Alice say she would lend me things. Even her earrings. Alice said earrings can make a person look terribly old. And I just might wear a hat. I never have, but I just might. This once!" She swiped at her hair.

"And of course clothes will help. I mortally despise clothes but I guess I'll have to. I heard Mollser say I'd get used to them. She said a persan can get used to anything and she sees no reason why I should be any different. I can't afford to be, Mollser said." Annie paused and looked down the empty street. She looked at the top of Galleons Lane, then looked hurriedly away. She wouldn't notice it. She would not even mention it. The night before was to be a time that had not happened. "I cut my nails last night," she said, and I knew then she was at last beginning to accept the situation created for her by others. Barker's biscuit factory advanced, and like a funeral, all she could do was let it pass. We walked up the street toward the bridge and the canal, and looking at her out of the corner of my eye I saw she had on today what was left of her confirmation dress. It was blue with puff sleeves and, even with the hem let down, ended just above her knees, scrubbed red this morning and marked with old scars.

At the bridge we stopped to look over into the locks below to see if anyone we knew had flung themselves into it during the night. But this morning it was empty. Only the water foamed and roared and tumbled. "Mollser says me wanting to be a dealer was one big joke," Annie said into it, and with her face dipped toward the water I couldn't see her eyes. "Maybe it was," she said. "Maybe it was never intended to be anything else. And maybe I should've known the whole thing was a great big fake. A great big fake all round." She was looking hard at the foam. I copied her. If you looked hard enough at something you could dim all the other things out. The foam of the water was made up of brilliant blue fluttering things. The spray settled and rose and gurgled. Watching, the trick was to focus on one single point in the wild waste.

"I suppose," Annie said, "you should go to Mass." She crossed her arms across her chest and pressed closer to the stone of the bridge.

"I suppose," I said; but this was a lip service we paid many a Sunday, hoping God would accept the thought for the deed. Looking up now I stared toward Rathmines, and from where we stood we could see the big fat dome of the Chapel. The thought of the Chapel and maybe meeting my Uncle Mick and my Aunt Mary rasped. When I got home tonight I would have to lie to my mother, but a thing like that no longer mattered. We came away from the bridge, crossed it, and went down the Rock Street side of the canal heading for Harecourt Terrace.

The houses, all private, were gray and, because the morning had not yet swelled, shuttered. We knew who lived in every single house. "If we meet anyone we know and they say anything about tomorrow we tell them nothing," Annie said. "I couldn't stand it for anyone to go on about it," she said. And I knew she meant me. We passed Lady Butler-Burke's house and next door the house of the actors who were great with her. They were two men, who walked the canal under the trees with books in their hands. One of them carried a walking stick. They both read from the books they carried; then, not looking at them, they would say what it

was they had just read out loud. On one side of the terrace
was a Home for the Blind, who were always early risers.

In the old days Annie gambled on the blind. "I'm taking bets," she'd say, and running past me would spread herself down on the grass opposite the flower paths where we
could watch the blind women trotting it out briskly. She
would then begin to call out odds like a bookie. If the first
two women walking toward each other missed, I lost to her.
If the second time round they met head on, I won. I never
understood why Annie was always the bookie; but she was,
or how she knew when to offer long odds; but she did. And
sometimes, with the really gullible she played The-Blind-
Meeting-the-Blind for pennies and often ended up with as
much as a shilling. "I've got a system," she'd say. And her
system had something to do with the angle of the white canes
the women used to get about with. But this morning, although the women were up and out as usual, she passed them
by without giving them as much as a glance.

At the end of the terrace she said, since it was early
for Sandymount we'd go first to Alexandra. It was a college
for girls and it was from here she took bikes. Sometimes to
make money by charging the kids round the street a penny a
ride; sometimes she took just for the hell of it, afterward
flinging the bike back down where she found it. Opposite
was the University. We crossed the road and tried the
middle doors of the University, but they were also locked
and so was every window in that long line of windows; and
then from long habit we headed for St. Vincent's Hospital
and the dead house.

Before Ellen Simms we went to the dead house every
Sunday morning. Sometimes on one of the slabs we'd see
someone we had known by sight or even to talk to. A young
girl maybe, wearing a blue shroud and Legion of Mary
medal, or an old man thrown careless with hands uncrossed

or a leg buckled under a flung sheet. Glowering then like a
hornet among headstones and her face stiff with indignation,
Annie would move to cross the hands, straighten the knee,
and condemn outright. "Them nurses and nuns for all their
eye-dropping and hand-covering are the right pack of hard-
faced bitches," she'd say. But today with only a nerve trembling across her mouth to set this Sunday apart from all the
other, she said: "I suppose you still want to go to the dead
house?"

I looked at her sharply. At her face seared by sun
across nose and cheeks, then at the untamed hair ragged
and black, ambushing the face; and I sought the change or
changes I had sensed earlier. Like her passing the Home for
the Blind and the blue confirmation dress. But nothing
showed. Nothing strayed. Yet I had the feeling I was being
weaned. Like a baby from the breast. Away from the known,
the loved. Of being left astray. But on her face nothing
showed. It remained smooth, calm. Its promise unblemished,
unchallenged. But still there was a difference, a containment
about her this morning that was not there before. An indefinable alteration in the face that I knew she would carry
with her always.

I made the desired denial. "No, I don't want to go to
the dead house," I said. "Let's see where *they're* going!"

To hide my own strange tension I turned and pointed
to a gang of kids milling down the lane where the dead
house and the Dispensary was. We followed and saw them
go into the Dispensary and heard inside others laughing.
Sitting at the door was a bull of a man behind a table, and
as each kid passed they gave him a card. We asked a youngwan whose face was hidden under the concealing brim of a
boater, what was up, but as Annie said, she was a poor
squint-eyed thing and wouldn't answer.

"An you know why," Annie asked loud: "Because legs

eleven is afraid what's going mightn't be enough for her."
And the youngwan, full of her own importance, swept up
the steps past us.

But at the door she turned back and said, "It's a party,
if youse must know."

"And you have to have a card," a youngfella with
glasses told us, "or you can't get in."

And we hadn't cards. "But we're getting in," Annie
muttered. But without cards, the joker on the door would
be unmovable. Men on doors always were. I remembered
Snakehead. "There'll be jelly and custard," Annie said.
"And I bet Maggie Hyland will be there."

And in the lane the kids stopped coming—because they
had all come, hundreds of them. Then we saw the man at
the table get up from it and go into the Dispensary, and the
minute the door closed on him we darted up the steps. He
had left the cards the kids had given him in neat piles, and
without pausing Annie grabbed two and knocked. The door
was opened by the same man. Annie held out her card to
him. He took hers but looked me over.

"You didn't have no card before," he said.

"He did so." Annie's face was blank, ageless. "But if
you must know," she said, "we're waiting for a friend."

"Well, where is your friend?"

Annie gazed blandly past him as if searching. "I guess
Miss Maggie Hyland is here already," she said.

"How old are *you?*" the man asked, and peered close.

"Ten," Annie said. "And as straight as an arrow," she
added, and she was now on for a laugh. "And although you
couldn't tell by just looking at me, I've shot up some in the
past three weeks. In fact," she said, "my dearest friend Miss
Maggie Hyland calls me 'Hand-me-down-a-star,' so that
should give you some idea how much I've grown."

"And that's the only idea it gives me," the man said

and leered and stared and sucked his teeth. But Annie, holding her ground, matched him stare by stare; then he took
my card and jerked his head.

Inside, long tables with white cloths ran the full length
of the Dispensary. On them tubs of ice cream and cakes,
stacked, made foothills over which the eye flew and the
senses reeled—hindered only by the smell of alcohol, ether,
and blood. White-smocked nuns and nurses rustled, waiting
hand and foot on kids who ate and collogued cakes and
sandwiches to take home. Huge glass bowls of Vimto flashed
and smouldered red in the light coming from windows up
near the ceiling—and backing them, pyramids had been
made by cunning hands out of oranges and apples. Urns
steamed tea and glasses bragged white with good thick milk.
And a nun, pale and freckled, gave out smiles with paper
hats. Some of the kids who had seen us hanging round outside looked knowing and acted fresh until we put them in
their places. We were a bit bigger, maybe a bit older, but
not that much bigger or older; yet today for some reason
they seemed a lot younger, or we a lot older; especially when
a culchi nurse came over and questioned Annie.

"And how old are you?" she asked.

Annie faced her. "Ten," she said.

The nurse gave her a look. "Aren't you going to wear
your hat?"

"No, I'm not going to wear my hat," Annie said, and
handed it back to the nurse. "This is kid stuff," she said to
me. "Let's go."

"Where to?" I asked.

"Sandymount."

Outside in the lane she aimed a piece of orange peel
back at the joker on the door. "Right between the eyes,"
I said. And we ran to Sandymount.

At Sandymount the tide was out and the beach crowded.

At a house near it we borrowed a bucket of water and a match from a servant and took it onto the beach, then gathered paper and twigs and lit a fire, and with the bucket on the boil, Annie went along the people and took orders for pots of it at a penny a pot.

We were needing a refill when the servant came from the house, and with bitter complaints took the bucket from us. "It's all black," she complained and Annie, reluctant to let the bucket go, asked her what she expected. Scanning the beach and the people crowding it, she said, "Know something: this is going to be a long hot day and there won't be a man, woman, or child on this beach who won't be wanting buckets of tea before it's out. Maybe we could get the lend of another bucket!"

"Who from?" I asked, and almost sore was my sudden longing for the moment to stay. But she shattered it.

"Wait," she said, looking hard at this woman with a large soup-can sitting near us. We got up and went over, and Annie offered her a sixpence for the can, or a lend of it, but the woman refused to sell. "This world," Annie said, looking straight at her, "is just about as full as it can be of real mean people." We waited, but the woman just crossed one leg over the other, outstared me, and eyed Annie coldly.

"What'll we do now?" I asked.

"Count our money," Annie said, and did, on the sand, and divided the three shillings we had made equally between us.

"Let's go to the tower," I said, for at the tower you could swim bollicky.

Annie shook her head, then said, "If you want." But at the tower instead of stripping she sat down and looked past me to the hill of Howth in the distance.

"Aren't you getting in?" I asked.

She shook her head.

"I've no knicks."

"You never have," I said. But she went on squinting hard at the sun. I stood looking down at her.

"You swim in the canal without knicks," I said, and she did, naked like the rest of us.

"I know, but Mollser says now I'm developing it's not right. Says I'm not to swim in my skin any more." She sounded defensive. "But you go, an I'll paddle."

I sat down beside her and out of the corner of my eye saw her take something from the pocket of her dress. I didn't turn to see what. I just sat and felt naked and left out. I saw a seaward-moving ship skirt Howth Head and went with it desolately floating over miles and miles of perilous oceans. Years from now, years and years, a ship like the one I was looking at would take me from here and from where I wanted to stay to places whose names Annie and I had stumbled over in Ellen Simms' books. And then beside me Annie laughed and looking I saw she had a lipstick in her hand and that her lips were red with it.

"It's Alice's," she said, and her eyes, clear as rainwater, had a look in them I'd never seen before. The expression was conniving grown. . . . She leaned toward me.

"Kiss me," she said.

"Why?" I asked, because through all those years I never had. Much as I wanted to I never had.

"You're supposed to."

I bent across and very carefully put my mouth to hers. It was soft and greasy. I drew back.

"Nothing happened," she said, and she was all surprise.

"What should?"

"With lipstick on, a person should shiver like they have a fever. Alice told me. But I didn't. Maybe we didn't do it right. I'll put some more on." She flattened her lips, and drew the lipstick across them.

"Try now," she said and held her face toward me again. I did. Then drew back.

"That didn't make me shiver none either," she said.

"Why do you want to?" I asked.

She shrugged, put the lipstick back in her pocket, and wiped her mouth with the back of her hand.

"You're supposed to want to," she said. "All girls are supposed to."

"But only proper girls," I objected. I remembered the sad gray-eyed girl long ago in Henry Street. Girls like her I thought. Girls who wore clothes. Who wore shoes. Who put ribbons in their hair. Who wore fur hats.

"I am a proper girl," Annie replied and let her glance fall on the bay again and across it Howth floating dreamy.

"If you ask me," she said, "it's just another fake. Another fake like all the others." I stood up.

"Are you getting in?" I asked, but she shook her head without looking at me.

I took a running header into the sea and stayed till I was blue, coming out only to hurl myself back in again but never coming close enough to be subjected to a scrutiny which I for some reason dreaded, but which Annie for some reason never made. Until:

"If you want my candy opinion, you better come out," she said finally. "You're turning blue, an if you don't believe me just have a dekko at your diddies." She didn't change her position, just sat hugging her knees and all the time looking past me as she spoke.

"I'm not coming out," I said, and dived under the water again.

"All right then. If you won't."

I heard her words, and when I looked again she was gone. I saw her walking skinny and fast along the beach making for the city. Damned if I'd shout. I ran out, dressed, and with my identity restored, ran after her. We walked home by way of Donnybrook. The streets and roads were half deserted and, after the day, baked. On a patch of a path, overripe mulberries from a tree in the garden fell. Feet had walked them into the path. It was stained black. Black as ink. . . . I thought Annie would stop to collect to sell, but she didn't. It was too late for that kind of effort now. She just looked up at the tree at the house as if she was taking a look at something she wanted to remember. As we walked she sometimes wiped sweat from her upper lip and every now and then rubbed the back of her hand across her mouth in a troubled way. Silence came between us. And so did something else. Some vague awful thing was straddling the air like a ghost hanging on thread. Something grim and secret as death. And again I felt locked out and alone and in peril. I braced myself for anything that might happen, positive that something would—but nothing did. And then I tried to make something happen. A couple of times I tried speaking Once about the roads we were walking on and the lanes off them, all of them loved and familiar in all weathers, in all seasons. And once about Ellen Simms. But she wouldn't answer. She seemed too preoccupied for conversation. She did, though, once and for no reason say:

"Us we just met on the canal one day: We didn't plan it or nothing. And we made no packs with each other did we? No promises. We never made no kind of—" she said, and her voice collapsed, a tenseness, a tight almost frightened tenseness seized her face, and she never spoke again. She did, though, after long coaxing join in a big game of Relievo that had begun round the top of Rock Street and the bridge when we got there. Every kid in the street was in it, and from the looks and size you could tell it would go on for hours.

"Let's get in," I cajoled, and together we went in; but somewhere in the game she went home without saying. And without her and missing her, the last of the last disappearing day halted abruptly, and on the bridge and, on me alone, the night closed in.

"I don't care who you hate, or who it is you're learning to hate," Mrs. Murphy said. "All I'm interested in right now is you getting them shagging feet of yours in the order God intended. Just put one foot in front of the other. It's all I'm asking. And I want to hear no more of your cants or hooring allegations or I'll swing for you."

Mrs. Murphy was standing on one side of the table, facing Annie on the other. Annie's hair had been curled up with a tongs and she had on the blue dress from yesterday— but overnight somebody had added a darker band to it to cover her knees. In her hands she had a pair of shoes. They were high-heeled patent leathers and belonged to Alice. She was holding them up over her head when I opened the door, and now she held them out to me.

"Three times," she said, "I've gone round this table and I still can't walk in these things!"

"Well, go round it a fourth time," Mrs. Murphy said, "and remember while you're doing it that this is a highly serious day—and if that youngfella there comes back to this house tonight with a job and you find yourself without one— don't even bother to darken this door because if you do I'll strangle you. Do you hear me?"

"I hear you," Annie said, "and so I'm sure does everybody else in this whole lane."

"Good," Mrs. Murphy said, "because it'll save me having to repeat meself—to you or them. An as for your learning to hate me? Well there's no love lost. And while I'm at it, I may as well tell you I don't intend to spend what's left of my life down on me bended wans doing novenas to an uncaring God just because you happened to be born a liar and peculiar."

"What do you mean, a liar?" Annie asked, looking hard at her mother.

"Exactly what I say," Mrs. Murphy snapped. "You've been out of that milk job for three whole weeks without my knowing."

"So you didn't go short, did you?" Annie asked. "You didn't have to do without your money?"

"That's true, I didn't," Mrs. Murphy admitted. "But I don't know where that money came from."

"And you don't care," Annie said.

"No more I don't," Mrs. Murphy cried, "an maybe I ought to," she sneered. "But I'll tell you," she said, and leant her full weight on her hands turned into fists on the table: "What I don't want this lousy Monday morning is you or your peculiarities ballsing up your chances below in Barker's. Just you remember that.

"And leave your Goddamned hair alone!" she screamed, when Annie, with a groan, racked her fingers through it. "Stop shagging well tearing at yourself. What do you want to do—make yourself a laughingstock and look odder than you already do in front of all them girls and fellas that'll be down there this morning?"

"Who in the name of Christ cares how she looks?" Mr. Murphy muttered from the bed.

"I care," Mrs. Murphy replied, and Annie gave her a sharp narrowed glance and held her in it till Mrs. Murphy said: "And so will you care how she looks if you find your-

self having to exert or put pressure on them bed muscles
you've developed over the years."

She paused and turned back, but in her glare Annie
could only see a reflection of her own lost face. "Just this
once," she said, and her glance went past Annie, "try to
behave like everybody else. Just try not to look like a bomb-
thrower dodging and twisting in and out of a crowd. There
are no shagging banners in your hands, so stop looking as if
there were. Just look good."

She moved round the table to Annie who was staring
at her with tense eyes as if willing her mother to look into
them. But Mrs. Murphy didn't; instead, looking at some
point to the left of Annie, she said: "Stand back a bit, and
get them shoes on." She held out a rag of a coat, that after
a slight hesitation Annie slipped into, then took the parish
priest's reference from the cluttered mantelpiece and gave
that to her.

"What you gotta remember," she said, "is you're a
regular girl grown and that any day now you'll be starting
to menstrate—and that a certain party who shall be name-
less is dead and so is all them queer and high-faluting notions she filled your head with—the summer is over and this
morning has manifested, just as I told you it would manifest.
And nobody—least of all me—gives a tinker's curse who
you hate, or how much you hate that factory: and neither
does it matter what, or who, it is you have to do to get that
job as long as you get it. And that's all I have to say on the
subject. And that's all the advice any good mother could
give you!" She opened the door, then closed it again, leaving Annie and me standing in the hall.

"I never thought I could hate anybody but I was
wrong," Annie said. "I'm learning. I'm learning real fast."

She bent, and with one hand pulled tighter the nylons
hanging loose round her thin ankles. I remembered Miz

Robey and her advice to Annie that day on the canal. "One day," Miz Robey had said, "when you've stopped feeling and learnt to hate a bit. When you're wanting a way further on from where you're bound to find yourself. Then if . . ."

"What will I do with these?" Annie asked, and held out the shoes in her hands. "I can get them on all right but I don't know how to walk in them."

"Put them on again and I'll hold you." She did, and taking my hand walked a couple of steps, then gave up.

"Oh Christ, I've got to," she cried, her head rearing in vexation, her face smothered with cheap white powder, her lovely mouth a bizarre gash of lipstick.

"You can't ask for a job in your bare feet," I said. "I'll tie them on with twine."

"We have none," she said, and stood there bewildered and wide-eyed. But I had twine—I always had twine in my pocket—and drew it out. And when she put the shoes on again I tied them to her feet.

"Try now," I said. She tried cautiously, one foot first, then the other. "Don't look down," I said. She shook her head. We heard in the distance the horn go in Barker's for seven, and when it stopped Annie was still on her feet, holding onto my arm.

"I've just got to," she muttered through clenched teeth.

"If we go slow," I told her. Her eyes now were slits of fury.

"I've got to go faster than this," she complained. "You hold me."

I nodded, and after a while I felt her grip lessen, and finally getting the hang of it she only caught me when a heel gave under her. "I wonder who the joker was invented these," she said, and other girls, hustling past, stared at us. A few braved a laugh but Annie only glared at them, then at me, and then down at her feet mashed flat in the shoes.

"They are *crippling* me," she said, but she kept going, and when we got to within a few yards of the door of Barker's biscuit factory I bent and undid the twine.

"Try now." And she did, but with grim and quivering lips, and bent at the belly as if nursing some terrible hurt.

"I dread going into that place," she said, and for seconds we stood silent, uncertain, unwilling to draw away from each other.

"Maybe it won't be too bad," I said, but she didn't answer. "If you don't straighten up they'll think you're sick," I warned.

"I am," she said. "I'm mortally sick."

I said: "Ellen Simms said a person should always embrace the unknown in a hurry!" She looked at me as if she was drowning but said nothing and at the factory's door took her hand off my arm.

Inside the door was a vast cavern of dark that pressed down heavy. Beyond it a long passage was lit by bulbs jailed in cages high in the ceiling. Under them, coaxing quickness into their tired bodies and faces, about fifty girls and fellows mixed. Against a partition and a door marked "Office" the more lusty bunched and turned shivery faces to us to see what it was they were up against.

"Who do you see here?" I asked a fella near us, but he didn't answer; but a girl near him, standing with her eyes half closed, spoke drowsy and said, "Miss O'Neill, the forewoman."

We waited, and after a time a woman wearing a blue overall came out of the office and the people leaning against the walls immediately pushed themselves from it. With bulgy eyes she stood and stared at the crowd, and then she began. "First of all," she said, "we want no chiselers here." She paused and then said: "Kids under fourteen can go." Nobody went. I could hear Annie's heart pound hell inside her ribs. "So nobody's under fourteen?" the forewoman said, and waited testing. "Okay," she said, and gestured to the girls. "You lot! I want youse to stand in line with your faces to the wall."

The girls turned and she began to walk along them, pulling roughly at the upturned collar of a coat and sweeping aside hair tumbling round necks. She was looking for something. But what? In a whisper I asked a fella standing beside me.

"Nit marks or the evil smear of a bedbug," he said and winked.

And along the line the forewoman went with a merry energy that wasn't in the least bit merry, and finally she had come to the last of the girls and Annie. Turning just as the forewoman reached her, Annie looked into her face. The woman opened her mouth as if to bid Annie to turn her face to the wall, but seeing what I saw she changed her mind. Confronting her the forewoman saw wide eyes, their irises stretched to a pale rim round the black, hard-shut white lips and dilated nostrils; a blazing rage, battened down by silence like the core of a furnace. For one second I thought the containment would break and that Annie would fly in, and the same thought musta crossed the forewoman's mind, for foregoing the examination she had given the others she stepped back.

"All right," she said, and with her gaze still locked with Annie's she stretched the "all" as far as it would go.

"Now what I want youse to do is stand with your backs to the wall and your hands out in front of youse. I want them fingers opened and spread apart," she said. "And you know why? Because I'm looking for itch or signs of itch and if I come across it I will touch that girl on the shoulder and

she can go." She went along the line and here and there she
touched a girl and that girl with flaming face ran up and out
past us.

"It's fucking well degrading," the fella beside me said
just as the forewoman, coming to the last of the girls, swung
round and looking at us said, "You fellas can beat it. We've
nothing for you."

"Why the hell didn't you say so in the first place,"
someone said; but my mind wasn't on him. It was on Annie
and so were my eyes. I looked at her. At her lips sucked
clean of lipstick. The blotched powder and the skin tanned
showing through. And I waited for her to turn and walk out
with me. But she didn't. She stood her ground. I saw the
forewoman beckon to her and saw Annie turn to follow and
then pause to look back. I stared and saw her give me the
smile, that terrible bit of a smile grown-ups throw kids when
they want to pacify or cheat—then drawing herself upright,
I saw Annie go with her head high through the door marked
"Office."

I'll wait, I thought. And remembered her father telling me that one of these days I'd be left waiting for Annie
if I wasn't careful. And with no warning I was suddenly
trying to retreat from a feeling that was riddled with pain.
She won't get the job, I told myself. She'll not pass the
doctor's test. Her teeth were bad. But they weren't. Annie
hadn't a bad tooth in her head or a blemish on her body.
And she had a lovely body. But she *was* ignorant. She
couldn't read or write her own name. And she had a bitch
of a temper. That forewoman had only to look crooked at
her and she'd be stuck into her right away.

I walked out into the street and waited and watched
girl after girl appear, but no Annie. That's because they are
giving her a good going over, I thought. They might even
be asking her to spell. If they did, that would finish any

chance she had of getting the job. That would put the kibosh on her and her mother. As in a dream I heard my name being called and called, and looking up at a window over the door I saw her looking down at me. I expected her to signal for me to wait, but she didn't. She just stared her black moody stare at me, then turned away and the window was empty again.

"She got the job," a girl told me, severing from me an irreplaceable part of myself, letting it loose like a kite on a broken string. "Your friend. She told me to tell you not to wait."

I didn't. I walked away. Back up Wexford Street I went into Camden, heading for the canal. In Charlotte Street I could smell autumn in the distance. Sense the beginning season's vague discontent. "The heart's ache must be resisted." So bollix the heart. "But these are the rules of the game that must be played." I know. I know. But some things come to life of their own accord. And then what do you do when the heart *screams* and persists in *screaming* its own rebellion.

Paul Smith
The Countrywoman £3.50

'The sensibility is true, the passion genuine. Mr Smith's gift for rendering speech is astonishing... When every drunken Dublin writer is a genius I don't feel like committing myself to the word; but I am sorely tempted' ANTHONY BURGESS, OBSERVER

'No novelist among the Irish has faced our slums – slum psychology, slum insanity and slum truth as Paul Smith faces them. He writes with fury, with mockery, with deadly accuracy; and with the most bitter and unflinching love. This wonderful book... a great achievement – it touches the heart, startles the conscience and does not leave one's memory' KATE O'BRIEN

'For his ability to write of such unutterable sadness with detachment, with the riotous humour of the Irish gutter, and without self-pity, Paul Smith deserves to be saluted by all men of his profession' NEW YORK TIMES

'Smith can combine black terror with riotous hilarity, rather in the way that O'Casey can do it. I realize that to put a writer's name on the same page with that of Sean O'Casey is giddily high praise. But now I think it is time for it' DOROTHY PARKER, ESQUIRE

'Smith has been compared to O'Casey and Joyce... I'd like to add to the list by suggesting that of Dickens and Dostoievsky' IRISH TIMES

'A rugged and shattering addition to English literature' Guardian

This and other Picador books are available at your local bookshop or newsagent,or can be ordered direct from the publisher. Indicate the number of copies required and fill in the form below

....

Name_____
(Block letters please)

Address_____

_____

Send to CS Department, Pan Books Ltd,
PO Box 40, Basingstoke, Hants
Please enclose remittance to the value of the cover price plus:
60p for the first book plus 30p per copy for each additional book
ordered to a maximum charge of £2.40 to cover postage and
packing
Applicable only in the UK

While every effort is made to keep prices low, it is sometimes
necessary to increase prices at short notice. Pan Books reserve the
right to show on covers and charge new retail prices which may
differ from those advertised in the text or elsewhere